MW01488319

Part-Time Worker, Full-Time Lover

Loved as a woman, married in a Fairy Tale

By Merry Goodman

#1 in the series: Love Me Forever

Part-Time Worker, Full-Time Lover © Merry Goodman

The right of Merry Goodman to be identified as the Author of the Work(s) has been asserted by her in accordance with the Copyright, Designs, and Patents Act 1988.

All rights reserved. No part of this publication may be reproduced, stored in or introduced into a retrieval system, or transmitted, in any form, or by any means (electronic, mechanical, photocopying, recording, or otherwise) without the prior written permission of the copyright owner.

This is a work of fiction. Names, characters, places, brands, media, and incidents are either the product of the author's imagination or are used fictitiously. Any resemblance to an actual person, living or dead, events, or locales is entirely coincidental.

The author acknowledges the trademarked status and trademark owners of various products referenced in this work of fiction, which have been used without permission. The publication/use of these trademarks is not authorized, associated with, or sponsored by the trademark owners.

All rights reserved. Copyright 2021 by Merry Goodman.

Cover designed by Rebeca of rebecacovers on www.fiverr.com

Table of Contents

Praise for Merry Goodman Romances

I just read another one of Merry Goodman's charming romances, *Encounter in Nashville.* This one took me back to my dating years and brought back memories of what it was like to be young and in love! Well written, Merry will keep you captivated.

Lady Margot

This story, *Recipe for Love,* is very sweet with Maria and Michael going through the same emotions, not wanting to be apart. They had great chemistry in all areas, and I love the communication they had. They meshed together, and I was drawn into the story. Merry, I like your writing style, and people get her stories!

TeeLovesSweets

Merry Goodman amazes us again with another innocent romance, *Girls' Weekend.* She always seems to include many elements that create a pleasing atmosphere. Not just a fulfilling romance, there are descriptions of good food, cute animals, and more that bring happy thoughts to the reader. I highly recommend this book!

Lady Margot

I love your book, *Girls Weekend.* You're an amazing romance writer. I can learn a lot from you.

Marloes Luppes, Author

In *Bad Date Redeemed,* Claudia's date from hell is saved by Allen, and they immediately click. Love blossoms and they quickly realize they were meant to be. This is a very charming and sweet read!

Callie D. Sutcliffe

This book, *North to Alaska,* is a sweet romance with a slow build. A great short read for those who love short, clean romances. I highly recommend this book.

Cindy Mendelson Klauss

I'm so glad you found inspiration from the cruise you took! I was hoping you'd write a cruise romance, *North to Alaska,* and I really enjoyed reading it.

Ameryn—My Copy Editor

A very sweet story, *Recipe for Love,* and will satisfy those who like love at first sight and happy endings.

Melanie Lambert - Author

I think the title of this book is right on target, *Recipe for Love,* because this is a clean sweet instant love story. I found it satisfying like a piece of fine chocolate; it was smooth and melted with warmth. Listen, I'm an action, horror, thriller guy, so take it from me, this was out of my comfort zone, but I truly liked it. It reminded me of a pleasant dream that makes you not want to wake up.

Barton Mann - Author

It might be silly to some people, but I'm thankful for sweet romances that can lift my spirits. So, as a reader of yours, thank you.

Stephanie B, one of my Beta Readers

Acknowledgments

A fiction story may be the invention of a single mind, but the publication of a book for others to enjoy involves many.

Stephanie B, and Victoria Seymour helped me as Beta Readers. They proved invaluable in forging my story into a better one.

Horus Proofreading (Angel Nyx) served as my proofreader, doing me an immense service in polishing my manuscript.

The cover design was by Rebeca of rebecacovers on www.fiverr.com. She did a marvelous job taking elements of my story and fabricating a cover with them.

Final thanks go to Tamara Nelson, my muse, who was invaluable in the writing and refinements of the manuscript. Without her encouragement and support, my Hippocrene, this book would not be in your hands.

Part-Time Worker, Full-Time Lover

Part-Time Worker, Full-Time Lover

Chapter 1

Norman

N orman's phone rang at 5:02 a.m., waking him from a sound sleep. His half-speed brain thought, *What day is it? Ah, yes, Wednesday.*

On the other end was his assistant, Carol, croaking at him about flu in her whole family, kids, Tom, and now her. Sighing, he knew what would come next. She would not be in today, and probably out the rest of the week.

Norman sank back into his bed after she hung up, pondering his situation. Mable at "Hire a Temp" would be his next call, to see if she had someone who could help for a few days, at least until Friday to get this project finished for the presentation next week. Ugh.

This year is a bad one for the flu. So far, I'm unscathed, but who knows what might happen. Better get up and get going.

He loved Petoskey, Michigan, in the fall, and he loved that he lived above his office. Converting the basement and first floor of his 1920s home into an office, he renovated the upper floor and attic into his residence. It was not a lot of space, but enough and it was close to work.

After a shower and breakfast, he went downstairs and fired up his computers to review the project, a major renovation of one of the famous lake houses from 1902. He needed help, desperately, and thought about how to divide it into temp-manageable tasks. Carol's absence was a major blow to progress, as she knew the project inside and out.

The clock rolled around to seven-thirty, and he took a chance that Mable would be in the office early. She answered on the third ring.

"Mable, my darling, how are you on this fine fall morning?"

"First, I'm not your darling, and second, I got almost no sleep last night due to the flu among my family. It's awful, and I fled my house to get away from them."

"Yes, it is, which is the reason I'm calling. I need a temp for the rest of the week who has computer skills. Do you have anyone?"

"Yes, I do. Christie Yaeger. She's excellent with a computer, and I can send her by nine this morning. Will that work?"

"Fantastic. Send her ASAP and thanks a million."

"Will do. Don't you want to know her rate?"

"No. I'll pay whatever. I just need ten fingers and a brain."

"She has those in spades."

"Excellent. Send me your bill. I'll use her through Friday for sure, and review the situation if Carol comes back next week."

4

Part-Time Worker, Full-Time Lover

*****

Norman

Right at nine, a woman knocked on his door. He sized her up through the glass, late-twenties, slender, well-dressed, pretty face, relatively short blonde hair, striking blue eyes, not curvy, but he liked her feminine looks. She wore a white scoop neck top and khaki pants, moderate heels, silver hoop earrings, and an agate necklace, not too long. What was most striking about her was her bright red lipstick. Her face just popped as a visual, which he appreciated. He opened the door, and she stuck out her hand, "Hi, I'm Christie Yaeger."

Her voice was low and pleasing, pleasant, not squeaky. This woman attracted him already, more than a little.

*****

Christie

Christie sized him up—mid-thirties, nicely dressed for the office, strong face and build, full head of hair, with some jawline facial hair, and a thin mustache, a bit taller than her, but not too much. He wore an expensive-looking watch. Into her mind zipped, *I can work with this guy, no problem.*

As they shook hands, a tiny spark passed between them when their fingers touched, bringing their eyes together.

Hmmm. A spark. Must be static electricity.

"Hi. I'm Norman Peale, and I am glad to see you. Please come in, and I'll tell you about my situation."

"Norman Peale? Are you related to that famous guy, the positive thinking one?"

Shrugging his shoulders, laughing, he said, "I'm asked that a lot and no, no relation at all."

Showing her to Carol's desk, he gave her log-in instructions.

"My two partners, Ryan and Edward, are out of town at their building sites. Mary and Tina, my two assistants, each called in sick on Monday and Tuesday. Carol is out as of five a.m. this morning, and it's just me, and now you."

She sat at the desk and logged into the computer using the Post-it that was there.

"The project is a 1902 lake house renovation for the new owners. I need you to evaluate the cost sheets to make sure there are no errors. Once that's done, I have more tasks for you."

He showed her where the files were, multiple sheets with many tabs for each kind of material.

"The house changed hands, and the new owner wants to update it and make it grand, taking it back to the glory days of early Petoskey. Amos, my friend, will be the general contractor and wants to start work in November. He'll work all winter inside, and then in the spring, will do the outside work and landscaping."

Listening, she said, "That sounds like a plan and thus the need to get these sheets done."

"Yes. Carol worked on them, but I got some last-minute changes in costs from Amos, and they need to be entered or fixed. Do you have any questions?"

"No, but I probably will. Let me look around at it."

"Okay." He pointed to his office. "I'll be in there if you need me."

*****

Christie

She started to work with the sheets and figured them out quickly. After about three hours she called for him to see what she had done. Emerging and pulling up a chair, he sat to review her work. She went through the sheets and pointed out fixes and other problems.

"I saw a closet on the second floor, which was not included in some costs."

"Yes, we discovered it, too, but didn't update the sheets. Glad that you included it where it was missing."

In her mind zipped, *He appreciates what I did,* and her heart beat faster.

"Also, I found some errors in the sums, the rows overlapped in some columns. I fixed those too, so the totals are right."

"Excellent. I was wondering about that but didn't check yet. Good catch."

A smile emerged on her face, reflecting her inner pleasure.

"Now that the basic sheets are ready, we need to put in the new costs from Amos."

Norman stood, hitting his palm with his fist.

"Excellent. What do you do for lunch?"

Christie turned her face upward to his. "Usually, I bring something, but Mable called me early, and I didn't have a chance to make it."

His hand thrust toward her, one finger vertical, signaling a thought.

"Not a problem. Let me order something from my friend's deli. We can eat here, as they deliver."

Nodding, Christie said, "Okay. Thanks for asking me."

He turned toward his office but turned back.

"Work on those cost changes until our food arrives, and then lunch is served."

"Okay. What do I owe you for lunch?"

His hands moved apart, horizontally.

"Nothing. It's on me for doing such a quick job getting those sheets ready."

"Thanks." She glowed inside—to be approved made her day. She worked hard to do a good job and win praise from her employers, even as a temp.

Lunch arrived, and they ate in the small kitchen. The deli name was on the bag. "Cormack's is my favorite deli," she said. "Their food is wonderful."

"Yes, I like it a lot too. My friend has done a good job with it."

They were silent for a few moments as they took the first bites, and he said, "So, tell me about your background."

"Well, I grew up as an orphan with my brother in foster care when he was ten, and I was six. My brother inherited our parents' house in Jacksonville, Florida, and I got the small summer house here

8

in Petoskey; I took possession of it when I was eighteen. Receiving a small inheritance allowed me to winterize my house and go to school at North Central, where I received an associate's degree in computer skills and business."

"You studied well."

"Yes, thanks. I enjoy it and am good at analysis."

"It shows."

His praise for her resonated in her and gave her joy. Finishing their food, discarding the trash, she asked, "What's next."

"You're quick. I thought it might take all day to get those sheets fixed. Next, we need a presentation of before and after from pictures and renderings to show the owner how the changes could appear."

"I can do that. I like to organize pictures into a presentation."

"Wonderful. Look in the same Dropbox area, one folder has pictures, and another has drawings. Look through them and select some, enough to make a compelling presentation, but not too long, perhaps thirty slides total, if that shows the whole outside. Put it together in PowerPoint, and I'll take a look when you're finished."

"Okay."

They separated, and she worked on her task.

There were lots of pictures, over one hundred, walking around the structure, and she had to organize them by what they showed, then consider the drawings to see how to match up the image angles. By five p.m., she was not done, but almost, having grouped the photo and drawing pairs for most of the structure but needed to finish the organization.

He emerged from his office, stretching his back. "Enough for today. You'll be back tomorrow at eight?"

"Yes. Mable said that I'm here through Friday."

"Excellent. You got a lot done today, way more than I thought. I'm very happy with how it's progressing."

Inside her, a gong sounded from his words. It reverberated all through her, and she smiled broadly.

"Thanks for saying that. I was glad to help. See you tomorrow."

*****

Norman

He watched her drive away in her older car, a RAV4 with rust.

Christie is an interesting woman. She bettered herself despite a terrible childhood and no resources. She's smart, organized, and a quick learner—what could she do if she had resources? I've never had a spark with a woman before. Can it mean something between us? Beauty describes her, and she attracts me. I'm glad she's coming back tomorrow.

*****

Christie

She thought about her tasks and his obvious pleasure in what she had accomplished.

This is a sizable project, and I made progress today. I've seen that house, and it will be grand when Norman gets done with it.

Christie paused in her thoughts as she drove.

And then there's the guy. I like his ways around me, getting me lunch, and letting me work without hovering over me. I like his looks, but I especially love his voice. The way he speaks is melodic to me. I wish he would read a book to me, so I could listen to him for hours. And his scent. I want to tackle him, hold him down, and just inhale him for half a day.

Christie was almost home, but couldn't give up these delicious thoughts.

And then, there's the spark. I've not had a spark with a man since I was a kid trying to zap Dad. Some of my girlfriends had a spark with their now husbands, and they're deeply in love, even after years of marriage and several kids. If this is a real spark, then it's serious. He might be my guy. Oh, my, I can hardly wait to see him tomorrow.

*****

Christie

Walking up to his door, she was ready for the day right at eight, as he requested. Today, she wore navy slacks and a sky-blue top, a different stone on a gold necklace, and several gold bracelets. She felt attractive. Rapping on the door, he opened it after a few moments. She extended her hand as an experiment—would the spark be back? As soon as their fingers touched, *zap*, stronger this time, drawing their eyes together, fixing them on each other for a moment.

Something is happening here. Perhaps something exciting for my future?

11

He welcomed her, and she logged onto the computer. Knowing that she needed to finish the PowerPoint presentation, she began immediately, saying, "I'll finish the presentation, and we can view it together, to see if it's what you want."

"Excellent. I'll be working on more renderings."

Working diligently, by eleven, she was ready. Like yesterday, he pulled up a chair, and she started the presentation. Thirty-two slides glided by, before and after, view after view, circling the structure and grounds. The images were mesmerizing. When it finished, he stood and applauded her. Like a firefly, she glowed from inside out.

"That's sensational. The client will love it, showing what we want to do with his house. You did a wonderful job."

"Thanks. I like the result. It shows what is and what can be."

"Yes, wonderfully. Great job."

"So, what's next?"

"Get into the email system and save as PDF's every correspondence from him and our response, as an electronic paper trail. Make sure we have responded to every request or thought of his. Make sure we've covered everything."

"Got it."

"Did you bring lunch? I didn't see one in your hand when you came in."

"No, I didn't make anything today."

"No problem, I'll order lunch from Cormack's again. Do you have a favorite?"

More time with him, yeah.

"Yes, I like the beef and cheddar sandwich. Maybe a cup of soup as well. You pick. I like everything from there soup-wise."

Thinking, he turned to his office. Popping his head out, he asked, "Horseradish on the beef?"

He considered my tastes. I like that.

"No, just some mayo."

Anticipating lunch, she bent to her task.

The food arrived, the sandwich she requested, and a cup of *Chicken and Wild Rice* soup. He had the same, but with ham on rye.

I love that soup; it's one of their best. He did well for me.

As they ate, she asked, "So I told you about my family. What about yours?"

"My father is a hedge fund president, and his firm does well. He is successful and thereby wealthy. But he inherited much of his wealth from my great grandfather, who was into oil and made lots of money in it. Some of that has passed down to me by my grandfather."

"Lots of money?"

Hesitating, he answered, "Yes."

"Like a million dollars?"

"Let's just say, lots."

"And, you live in Petoskey in a small house-office?"

"I like it here. I could be anywhere, but I chose here, mostly to be out of New York."

Considering their two-time spark, the thought whizzed through her, *I'm so glad you did.*

"Then, why are you working? You could be retired today, living an easy life?"

"I like my work. I went to school to learn how to design what I see in my mind when I look at something. I wanted to be able to bring it to fruition. Work is fun for me."

"What schools?" She imagined the best ones.

"Cornell for my undergrad degree and then Harvard for my master's."

She sat back, never imagining herself with someone who was the antithesis of who she was and from where she came. He had top-flight schooling and tons of money. She had two years at a local community college and no money. She pondered for a moment, then said, "How marvelous for you."

"I like my life."

Their food was finished. "How are you doing with the email trail?"

"Maybe halfway. So far, we've addressed every concern or thought of the client."

He smiled when she said, "we," a connection to him.

"Excellent. When you're done with that, call me, and I'll give you the next task."

About three-thirty, she finished and called him to consider what she did. He loved it, now confident that he had addressed every concern that the client expressed. Each client email had a matching response, and the e-paper flowed as the days flowed, easily identified. The organization was perfect and could be continued by the assistants. She gleamed with success.

With that concluded, he suggested that they quit for the day. Tomorrow would have more.

"I'm so pleased with our progress. Tomorrow we'll send the client an invitation to view the presentation next week."

Pleased with her day, he walked her to the door with his hand on her back, with tingles erupting where he touched her.

This is too good—two sparks and now tingles. Best would be for him to kiss me goodbye. Fat chance of that happening, but still, a girl can hope.

*****

Norman

He watched her move to her car and drive away, closing his door only after she disappeared. *I like this woman already. I love how she moves and carries herself, positive, confident. She's smart and catches onto a new task quickly. I wish she could stay and have dinner with me, so we could be together more.*

*****

Christie

Friday dawned with rain. She saw him watching her as she opened her car door and all the way to the entryway. To wait for her at his door pleased her. Sans lunch was also part of her plan to spend time with him. She settled in at Carol's desk, ready for her next assignment.

The day flowed by. Norman emailed the client regarding the proposal of seeing the presentation. He responded immediately that ten on Wednesday was good for him. He was eager to see what they envisioned.

They did more organizing and made material order lists for Amos. Ordering lunch for them again, they ate together, talking more about his university years. She wanted to know what it was like to attend Harvard.

By five, Norman was confident about the project and his preparations. He wanted to see the presentation again.

As the last slide faded, stretching his back, his arms overhead, he asked, "How about if we go out to dinner tonight, together?"

Chapter 2

Christie

S urprised, she turned to him. "Like a date? With you?" Her heart leaped for joy.

"Ummm. Yes. How about the Freshwater Grill?"

"They have the best whitefish in the area."

"Yeah."

Barely containing her joy, she tried to be nonchalant about it, to not seem desperate.

"Yes. I'd like that."

Might he have something more in mind, something romantic in his house? Like, sit by the fire and cuddle. Something that would make my night, my week, my month, and my year?

"Excellent. Then let's close this place down, and we can go."

He disappeared into his office as she shut her computer down. Joining him at his door, he put his hand on her back, tingles again, and walked her to another door, out the back to the garage. The door opened, and there were two cars, each the opposite of the other. One was a new Audi RS 5 coupe. She dreamed of riding in such a car, power and leather, and everything marvelous. Right next to it sat a very old car but in pristine condition.

"Which are we going to take?"

Thinking for a moment, he said, "How about the Model A?"

"Oooh, that would be fun."

They moved to her door, and he opened it for her; it squeaked just a little and sounded old. "This is a fun car, a 1930 Model A, deluxe roadster. My grandfather bought it, and he passed it along to my father, who drove it for years. When I admired it, he gave it to me when I was twenty."

Slipping into the driver's seat, he said, "I drove it some, but mostly I tried to preserve it. Period clothing adds to the adventure, and I drive it in parades, especially in the July 4th parade.

Christie's eyes widened, and she said, "I've seen this car in that parade. I had no idea it was you."

Laughing, he said, "One time, the high school prom queen wanted to ride in it to the dance. Obliging her and her date, she was the talk of the prom, arriving at the event in this classic car with me as her chauffeur."

"How fun."

To ride in this car was a thrill for her. She never imagined herself on a date with a man in this stylish a ride from yesteryear. Her mind swirled with scenes of what could unfold.

Arriving at the restaurant, he ran around to open her door and help her out.

How grand is this, how romantic, a spark twice, tingles when he touches my back, opening my door, helping me out. I feel so cared for as a woman.

Perusing the menu, they both ordered whitefish—the specialty of the house. His teen and college years were topics of conversation. "What was it like growing up with money, lots of it?"

"Well, of course, I went to prep school, even from kindergarten, driven there in a car with a family driver, but I went home every night. My parents didn't want me in boarding school. My classmates were our neighbors, some of them, but also from all over the city. It was like any school, we were kids and got into trouble, some more than others."

Christie laughed. "Preppy trouble-makers—who would have thought."

"In high school, there were lots of drugs, as the kids had money, but that was among the scummy crowd. I never got into their ways, as I wanted to study architecture from seventh grade. Drawings of buildings were my doodles. Frank Lloyd Wright was my hero."

Christie laughed, touching his arm. "Superman in his own way."

"Yeah.

"On a trip through Pennsylvania, I got to see one of his more famous houses, *Fallingwater*, southeast of Pittsburgh. My father made it a point to go there for me."

"What a great dad to do that for you."

"Yeah, he was. I had a good family life growing up."

Having already described her growing up with the lack of it, the opposite interested her. She could see that he was a little embarrassed in talking about it.

I like that about him, using money to get what he wanted but didn't flaunt it.

About halfway through dinner, her best friend Samantha and a girlfriend entered and sat about three tables away. Samantha came to whisper in her ear, "Look at you. Out on a date with a guy. Who is this?"

A quick, "I'll tell you later," then, when she didn't return to her table, Christie said, "Samantha, this is Norman Peale. Norman, this is my best friend, Samantha Ostenberg."

Shaking hands, Christie watched their eyes.

No spark. Good. He's mine.

Christie said, "I'm working for Norman as a temp while his assistants recover from the flu. It took out all three of them."

"Oh, my. That's terrible."

Not for me. I slid into home plate.

Samantha said, "Well, enjoy your dinner."

"Nice to meet you," said Norman as she turned away.

Samantha returned to her table but moved to a different chair.

She just wants to watch me with Norman. No spark, no problem.

They resumed eating, but after a few bites, he asked, "Are you doing anything tomorrow?"

"Why do you ask?"

"Well, I thought we might go to Mackinac Island and tour the fort."

Her posture straightened, and her eyes brightened, "I've never seen it."

"And then, lunch at the Grand Hotel?"

Two dates within twenty-four hours. This is fabulous.

"Tomorrow is open for me, so I'd like to go with you."

20

Excitement colored his voice. "Excellent, so, I'll pick you up at nine?"

"Yeah. Will we take the Model A?" She gave him a wry smile.

Laughing, he said, "No. The Audi is more comfortable."

"And, a lot faster."

"For sure."

Dinner finished, he paid and walked her to the car. It had collected a couple of admiring men. To be a passenger in the object of their fascination made her heart leap for joy. Norman opened her door and helped her in. The men continued to watch as he backed out and drove off. All they needed were yellow scarves and the top down. She loved it.

As they arrived at his house, she was almost embarrassed by her aging RAV4 in the front. He parked in the garage and asked, "Would you like to come upstairs for some wine and to sit by the fire?"

Sitting with a fire tonight and a fun date tomorrow. Does it get any better than this?

"I'd like that, but just half a glass, as I need to drive home."

His hand caressed her back. She expected tingles, but in their place was a sense of connection, him to her. She liked that better.

Leading her upstairs, she found a modern space in a hundred-year-old house. "You did a splendid job with this space."

"Yeah, I rather like it. This is the living area with a small guest room. My bedroom is upstairs in the attic. I'm away from everything when I'm up there."

Parting from her, walking to a cabinet, he asked, "Music with our wine?"

"Yeah."

'I have eclectic tastes, from the *Jonas Brothers* to classical and most recently, I've streamed Renaissance. It's melodious, simple, and to me, calming."

"I've never listened to it. I'm curious."

He chose the streaming station on his phone, which played through four speakers in his living room. A pair of lutes played a simple tune.

Sitting on the sofa by the fire, melodious music flowing around them, he opened the wine and poured. "I like sweet wines more than dry."

"Me too."

Tasting his choice, it was a sweet, flavorful liquid rolling around on her tongue, not biting her. He sat next to her and took her hand into his.

"Where do you see yourself in five years?" he asked.

Thinking for a moment, she responded, "That's a good question. I'm not a goal person. For years, I've tried to respond to the day's needs, and almost don't plan a week ahead except for appointments. I'm a true responder. What about you?"

"I'm a bit more goal-oriented than you, just from my work. I need to manage the money, which is entrusted to me, but that is more responding to market conditions. Personally, I'd like to be married, happily, and have children. I want to be a couple with my wife, like my parents were, desperately in love, connected and involved with each other, partners in life. And, I want to be involved with my kids, attending their events, with them in everything as they grow up."

Her heart leaped at what he said.

This is perfect. Could I be the object of his dreams?

They sipped and talked, sipped, and talked. With her half-glass of wine gone, they both were warm from the fire and relaxed. They had been sitting, but now they tipped over to lay on the sofa, spooned with his arm across her middle. She could feel his breath in her hair, and he sniffed the scent of her perfume and her hair as well.

Talking on for an hour, she whispered, "I should go, as we have an adventure tomorrow."

"For sure."

He sat up and stood, helping her stand, walking her down the stairs to the office and the door.

Turning to him, she said, "I had a wonderful time tonight. Thank you for asking me to dinner and then upstairs by the fire."

"It was my pleasure. I enjoyed being with you."

With their faces close, they entered into a kiss or no kiss dance. She would move toward him, then retreat. He would do the same.

He wants to kiss me but is afraid he's too bold, too fast.

A couple of dance moves later, he moved his lips to hers and his hands into her hair, holding her to him. She surrounded his neck with her arms and held them together as well. After some moments together, he parted, staring into her eyes. He moved to kiss her again.

Closing the distance, she responded eagerly, inhaling his scent, both man and perfume, a tantalizing combination. Moments connected elicited some soft moans from her. After more moments, he parted, close to her, eye to eye.

He likes me, more than likes me. I can see it and feel it in his kisses.

"I should go. Adventure awaits tomorrow."

He let her go with a caress of her cheek to her lips, touching them with his fingers.

*****

Christie

As soon as the door shut, Christie wanted to dance a jig. As she drove toward home, her mind whizzed.

We shared wine and a fire in his house. He held my hand as we sipped. We relaxed and lay together on the sofa, and we cuddled with his arm over me. Then, he kissed me, not once, but twice, not a peck, but a real kiss, passionate enough that I heard myself moan. I've not moaned from a man's touch in forever. Then his fingers moved along my cheek to my lips and caressed them.

Parking, she got out, unlocked her door, ran to her bed, and flopped on it, her mind still whizzing.

And, I have a date with this guy tomorrow, less than 12 hours away, for the day, not just dinner. Oh, my.

She ran through it all again, savoring each part. Their kiss she relived over and over, tasting him, sensing his lips on hers, sensing his hands in her hair and on her ears, caressing her.

Looking at her phone, she saw a text from Samantha, wanting to know everything, to call her the instant she was available.

Christie hit Samantha's name on her phone, and she answered on the second ring.

"So, tell me everything."

"His name is Norman Peale, and he's an architect."

"I know him. He drives a sporty old car, right? I saw it in the parking lot."

"Yeah. It was so fun to ride in."

"And, he has a boatload of money, right?"

"Yes, but he doesn't flaunt it too much."

"Uh-huh. And, he has had dozens of girlfriends and one fiancée, at least for a time. I read they broke up."

Christie was uneasy about where this was going.

"So, you're the current girl model who he's playing with before he throws you away?"

Her voice became defensive. "He doesn't seem like that. Samantha, you can't believe everything you read in those gossip columns or on the internet."

"Just wait. He'll chew you up like a piece of gum, and when you lose your flavor for him, he'll spit you out."

"Sam, why are you so negative."

"I'm trying to save your butt from pain and agony."

"He's not that way, at all, from what I see."

"Well, when you're on your bed, crying your eyes out, don't call me, because I warned you!"

Christie whispered, "I need to go. Talk to you later." The connection closed.

Thinking about what Samantha said, she rejected it as old news.

He seems way different from how Samantha sees him.

She rose, put her pajamas on, and got into bed, pushing aside Samantha's negativity.

He asked me on a date, and it was a fabulous one. And he asked me out for tomorrow for an all-day date. What's negative about that?

Her mind returned to savoring her dates, one tonight and one in the morning.

How fantastic is that, just what a girl wants. She paused. *But, what if Samantha's right?*

Chapter 3

Christie

C hristie heard him pull up, and she was almost ready to go. Norman came to her door and knocked.

So glad I tidied up.

Letting him in, she gathered her things. He looked around, and she knew he was sizing up her space with his architect's eye.

"Renovation would do a lot for this space, but it's nicely laid out."

A little embarrassed, she explained, shrugging her shoulders. "I know, but I have neither the money nor the time, though mostly the money."

Nodding, he responded, "I understand that. I have numbers of clients who wanted to remodel, then were surprised by the costs and reluctantly decided against it. Drawings were made, but they found no way to make it happen."

Exiting, she locked her door and stood, admiring the four-wheeled rocket ship before her, the top down. She had never been in so sporty a car, except perhaps last night in his Roadster. Helping her in, he started the engine. The rumble was amazing, so many horses under the hood, awaiting release.

He drove along Hwy 131 until it became four lanes, and after that, he unleashed his horses. To her, it seemed like a rocket launch, thirty to eighty in four seconds; the acceleration pressed her into her seat and brought out a big smile.

"This is a fun car," he called out over the noise of the wind.

With her hair flying and a happy face, she said, "Oh, baby. That it is. I wouldn't know how to drive it after my old RAV4."

"It's easy but takes some getting used to. It's a Quattro, so even in the winter, it goes through anything."

In short order, they arrived at the ferry terminal for a short wait, then a twenty-minute ride to the no-cars-allowed island.

A cart vendor sold smoked fish, Chub, among others.

Pointing at the offering, Norman said, "I've had this before, and it's good. Want to try it?"

"Sure."

Norman bought one, and they ate it with tiny plastic forks.

"You were right. It's good."

As they discarded the trash, the ferry arrived, and they boarded.

The ride to the island seemed quick, and as they docked, Christie asked, "Can we walk the shops?"

"How about this? Let's go to the fort and the tour, then to lunch at the Grand Hotel, then come back to the shops, so if we buy something, we don't have to carry it all day."

"Better idea."

The horse and buggy stand was nearby, and they engaged one to take them to the fort. Sitting together, he held her hand. No more romantic a way to travel existed than this; it even beat his Audi. Her heart fluttered.

Only better would be if he kissed me as we rode.

Waiting and hoping, she saw him move toward her, and she thought, *Does he read minds?*

He turned her face to his, and his lips slid on hers first, then he pressed their lips together, almost possessing her. A hand into her hair, he deepened their kiss, letting their tongues touch, as his scent wafted into her nostrils.

Parting just a little, she said, "Let's do that again." She pulled them together, her lips onto his. Worlds dissolve with such a kiss, his touch, his scent, and she reveled in being with him, close to him. They parted and sat back, glowing from their connection.

"Welcome to Mackinac Island," he whispered.

"I'm so glad I came."

"Same here."

Almost at the fort, they could see other buggies waiting. Their driver let them out and then joined the others, awaiting another fare. Entering the fort, they signed up for the tour, which began in twenty minutes, enough time to peruse the gift shop and take in the sights from the fort out to the water. A commanding view of the straits presented itself, any boat passing would be spotted, which was the intent of the fort. She took selfies to remember their trip.

At one of the cannons, Norman assumed the position of a gunnery officer. "Private, aim at the lead ship of those scallywags and fire when ready."

Christie snapped to attention and saluted. "Aye, Aye, sir." She stood at the cannon as if aiming it and shouted, "Boom. A hit, sir."

He pumped the air with his fist. "Good shooting, private. Reload and hit 'em again."

She pretended to pull the cannon back and reload from the pile of cannon-balls next to her but fell apart in laughter before she could shoot again.

The tour passed through most parts of the fort, giving them the history of it and the battles which happened there. At the flagpole, Christie announced, "Private, lower the flag for nightfall."

"Ma'am, yes, ma'am," responded Norman, pretending to haul it down the pole.

Blowing taps through her fist, she got halfway through the tune when laughter interrupted her.

At one of the walls, he pretended to hold a musket, shooting at invisible enemy soldiers. "Bang. Take that, you invading British scum." Turning to her, he said, "Reload, private."

He pretended to hand Christie the musket, with her laughing, saying, "I don't know how."

"Sure you do, private. Hand me the already loaded one in your hand."

She figured out his line of thought, tossing him the loaded musket, which he pretended to shoot again. "Bang. Missed the bugger."

Christie laughed again, saying, "I want a selfie of us repelling the invisible invasion." She took several, some serious ones and some with funny faces.

The guide explained that this fort had a very long line of communication to the command center, and the men stationed here rarely knew what was happening in the rest of the country, a war raging or peace.

They exited and engaged a carriage to the Grand Hotel, a leisurely ride, as this driver talked more than the first. He regaled them with the history of the Grand Hotel and the presidents and other dignitaries who came there, the most recent president being Gerald Ford, who played golf. Dropping them at the main entrance, Norman offered his arm.

Christie gasped with an idea. "I know. Let's imagine ourselves attending an elegant event. You're wearing a tux, and I have on a glorious evening gown, attending a magnificent ball with my husband. You adore me and give me the finest of everything."

Nodding, he straightened his back, his arm still offered. She gathered her dress to mount the stairs. Moving upward slowly for all to see their elegance, she tried hard not to giggle.

With a haughty accent, he said, "Darling, do you think we'll see the governor here tonight?"

"My love, I've already seen his carriage. He's inside, for sure."

"Good, I need to talk with him about the renovation of the Governor's Mansion."

"Will it be extensive?"

Flicking his imaginary cigar, he said, "Oh, yes. Millions. I love state money."

At the entrance, he pretended to be the doorman, bowing deeply.

Nodding to him, she said, "Thank you, James, for holding the door," hiking up her dress as she entered.

Both of them laughed at their antics.

Norman asked for a table that could see the golf course, resulting in one on a veranda. The menu was extensive, and they agreed to have different entrées and share bites. They passed a dessert cart on the way to their table with its scrumptious offerings. Save room for dessert should be an intent.

The food was exquisite and to watch the golfers, some capable and others not so, gave them added enjoyment. One guy hit a bad putt, flipped out another ball, and tried again, looking around first to see if anyone noticed.

Christie said, "I saw that. He flipped out a second ball to try again."

Nodding, Norman said, "Yeah. Old golfing technique. Use it all the time. And if he does better, that will be the score he cards."

Shaking her head, she murmured, "Golfers are a bunch of liars."

"Lots of times, yeah. Honor is a relative word to them."

Their meal finished, they took a carriage back to town and the dock. Norman took a picture of the boat schedule, so he knew how much shopping time they had.

"Can we get some fudge?" she asked.

"Sure. I've heard that it's the best here with lots of varieties."

They wandered the streets, entering a shop with many mementos. "See this model of the fort?" she said, picking it up.

"Yeah."

"I want to get it to remember our day."

"Great idea. I'll get one of the Grand Hotel."

Watching the time and having seen the shopping row, they strolled back toward the ferry. As they neared the dock, looking at the boats tied up there, they could see it in the distance. Once underway, they strolled to the bow, and stood like the couple in *Titanic*, facing the wind, arms out. He turned her and kissed her deeply, lingering, his lips on hers. Her world shrank only to him; he invaded her heart and soul with his romance.

Today was magical. I've never had a time with a man like today, where he lavished romance on me and ensured that our times were memorable. We have something going on between us, I can feel it. I can't imagine a better time with a man, except maybe him making love to me.

The trip to the mainland dock was quick, and soon, they were back in his car, zooming home with the top down. Early in the afternoon, he suggested, "How about coming to my house, have some wine by the fire, then make some dinner later."

"I'd like that."

I'm so glad he wants more time with me, not just drop me at my house.

Parking, he helped her out, and they walked to his door arm in arm.

This is marvelous, arm in arm with my guy.

Clicking the switch started the fire, and she sat on the sofa, awaiting him and wine. She scanned the room, taking in his furnishings and decorations.

The design is so well done, a place for everything, yet everything is easily accessed. No clutter, but attractive things which make the room look homey and well put together. That's his mind. I've seen it in his work and his drawings, now again in his house. I never have time to organize my house or money to make places for my things; rather, it's a jumble of convenience.

"Music?"

"Yeah. Mr. eclectic music, what will you choose for tonight?"

"Hmmm, how about some George Winston piano solos?"

"I've heard of him. He's fantastic on a piano, improvisational, right?"

"Yeah. Dad found him back in the 1970s. I think he started a genre of that style of piano music because Dad says that no one like him existed then. Now you can find a bunch of artists who play as he does. I attended one of his concerts, and he'd play a tune that I know from his recordings, but he played it differently, a tweak, improvising on the original score, which makes it interesting. He plays with no music in front of him, just a small piece of paper, a list of his selections for the evening."

Norman opened the bottle, poured, she clinked with him, and they sipped their wine. He took her hand into his, and they talked about their day, what was most interesting.

Christie pondered. "To me, the history of the fort was the most interesting. They had two battles during the War of 1812, and both were British victories. Ironically, the American commander from the first was killed by the British in Detroit as he was being tried for cowardice for surrendering. That's just awful."

"I agree. Back then, communication was so poor that they never knew what was happening elsewhere for months, if at all. They were on their own—do what seems best at the time."

The late-day sun streamed in the windows, and their wine was finished. Like last night, the fire warmed them, the wine relaxed them, and they lay on the sofa cuddled, spooned.

What could be better than this except for being married? Then, he could carry me to bed and take me past the moon, making love to me, just like in the romance novels. I'm with a man who could make it happen.

She said, "I googled you and found you're popular among the local women, and even among some not so local women. Did I see an engagement?"

"Yeah, there have been women. And, yeah, three years ago, I was engaged, to Cynthia, but it fell apart when she decided that she liked my best man better than me. There is no pain, like broken heart pain. For her, it turned out that he truly was the best man, not me. They're married now with a baby, and I'm happy for them. I didn't date at all until I recovered."

"That's pain to the max."

"It is. We're still friends on Facebook, but nothing else."

A little afraid to ask for more, she did, anyway. "So, no current girlfriend?"

"No, not for some months. My last one, Courtney, decided to move to California and become an actress after our breakup."

"Did she have any success?"

"She moved but has found no part yet from what I see on Facebook. Not even as an extra."

I'm glad she's that far away. Probably not a big risk if she returned. He seems over her. He keeps up with people on Facebook, even if they're out of his life.

"Facebook connections seem important to you."

"Yeah, as I like to keep up with people who have been significant in my past and Facebook works for that. I don't want

35

connection with them, just to see what they're up to and if they're headed my way. Then, I can cut off any involvement before it becomes awkward."

Glad to hear that. Keep them away.

They were quiet for a time, and then he said, "How about some dinner? Lasagna?"

"Does it take forever? I know a guy who spends three days making his."

"No, about an hour, including baking time."

"Wow. I love lasagna. Let me help."

"Okay."

He rose and offered her a hand up. Moving to the kitchen, he handed her a pound of ground beef, and a bottle of sauce, saying, "You fry the meat and add the sauce. I'll make the cream and get the rest of it ready."

In the kitchen, he would bump her hip, or snap a towel at her, and she would retaliate. Somehow a dollop of cream got onto her nose, and he removed it with his tongue, then kissed her. Each held cooking implements in their hands, so they pressed their lips together by leaning in, arms out. Moments later, they both laughed.

She whispered, two inches from his face, "I enjoy cooking with you."

"Yeah, me too."

They worked together to assemble the dish, then into the oven it went. He unwrapped some garlic bread from the freezer and added it to the oven after twenty minutes.

"Do you want a salad?"

"Yeah, that would be nice."

A bag of prepared salad dumped into a bowl, made it happen, and he added some decorations, taking it to the table. She found table settings and made the table ready.

"More wine?"

"Who would say no to more wine?"

"We might have to cuddle until you can drive home."

"Oh, darn. What a nightmare!" Hands on her hips, her face displayed a sly look.

He laughed as the timer dinged. Grabbing pot holders, he took the lasagna to the table, and she brought the bread. He poured wine—a sweet red this time—and offered her portions and took for himself. Tasting it, she smacked her lips. "Mmmm." She devoured hers and took more.

"You were hungry."

"Yeah, and this is so tasty. I love lasagna."

Finished, they sat back, sipping their wine, digesting. He took his glass, offered her a hand up, and said, "To the sofa."

Following him, she sat next to him, their feet on the table, savoring their evening.

After a time of quiet, he asked, "I have an adventure trip planned for the first week of October, Friday through Monday. It will be three nights in the lodge on Isle Royale at Rock Harbor, at the east end of the island. I plan each day to go on a hike and then back home. Do you have an interest in going with me?"

Sitting up, she turned to him. "That sounds fantastic. Let me check my schedule." She knew full well that nothing was there, as she did nothing and went nowhere, ever; her life had no adventure in it. Adventure costs money, and she had none.

Retrieving her phone, she opened the calendar app. On the first week of October, those days had no entries, empty. Looking over her shoulder, he saw the absence of entries, too.

With just a touch of sarcasm, she said, "Ummm, I'm not sure. My life is super busy, and my calendar is so full."

She tried hard not to laugh.

"But I think I can squeeze you in, soooo, yes, I'll go with you." She turned to him with dancing eyes, smiling.

Now, he laughed. "Excellent. It will be fun, and the fall colors might be near their peak then."

The wine gone, slowly they tipped over on the sofa, cuddled with his arm over her middle, caressing her softly.

"I like you here with me. I feel whole," he whispered.

Her heart absorbed that remarkable statement from him. It resonated with her own heart as she sensed the same in herself. However, Samantha's words floated into her mind, though she pushed them away. Snuggling closer into him, they let the music flow over them.

They cuddled for perhaps forty-five minutes, quiet, resting, at peace with each other. She whispered, "I should probably go. I have church in the morning, and I'm helping with the junior highs."

"That sounds like a challenge."

"Sometimes, but they're fun as well. We play games and then have a Bible lesson, stories which they act out many times. We have some skilled leaders, and I'm a helper."

"Okay. Do you know your work schedule for this next week?"

"No. Mable will send me a text on Sunday night what the week holds, except for a surprise, like you on Wednesday."

"I understand, and am glad you were available."

"Yeah, me too. Divine Providence."

She stood, and he walked her downstairs to his door. As they neared it, he turned her and kissed her with his hands in her hair, caressing her ears. Surrounding his neck with her arms, she held them together. Their kisses only got better; their tongues danced with each other.

He whispered, close to her ear. "I have a thought for Thursday afternoon. Are you available?"

Oh, I loved his thought of our Mackinac Island trip. I'm in.

"I'm sure that I am."

"I'll text you with details as we get closer. We can talk about the adventure trip then too."

"Good idea."

He kissed her again and let her out. As she neared her car, she called back, "I like your ride more than mine."

"At least it gets you from A to B."

"True, with no style."

When can we ride in the Roadster again?

*****

Norman

39

Norman watched Christie get into her car and drive away. Renaissance music continued to play, reminding him of their cuddle on the sofa, relaxed from their meal and wine.

Could marriage with her be like this? We've had so little time together; I've not seen her angry side. What would we argue about? What would she demand? We like a lot of the same stuff. Would we settle an argument, or would it drive a wedge between us, leaving painful splinters?

Norman still stood, staring blankly at the closed door.

That woman is getting to me. She's so easy to be with, so fun, we click together. For her to leave is like a piece of me just drove away, like a hole in my heart opened up when she left. I'm investing in her already. With some other women, I was glad when they left, but not this one. We've known each other for what, a few days, and already she's become part of me. How fantastic is that?

*****

Christie

For Christie, as soon as she started to drive, she relived her day, every moment, savoring the memories. She picked up her fort memento, reliving their kisses in the carriage, and on the ferry. Her mind whizzed with memories until she was home, on her bed, arms out, listening to streaming love songs, letting the music flow over her. The boring life which she lived before had now morphed into something exciting, filling her with joy and romance.

Nothing could be better than where this is going. Yet, could Samantha be right? That, I'm the flavor of the month? He keeps tabs on his ex-girlfriends. Could that be a problem? Could one of them waltz into his life, and he prefers her over me?

Chapter 4

Christie

On Thursday, Norman picked her up in the Roadster, top-down, and drove to Sunset Park, her hair flying in the wind.

This car is so fun to ride in. I love it.

The food was in a picnic basket, one of those high-end ones which had real plates and silverware. He carried it as they walked along the river, feeling the spray from the falls on their faces. Setting the basket down, he drew her to himself, wrapping his arms around her. He moved his face to hers and kissed her, holding her body to his. The roar of the falls disappeared, and all she sensed was Norman.

He parted, but she pulled him back for another kiss.

Not done yet.

Her mind reveled in their connection. Starved for romance and male attention, now that she tasted it, she wanted more.

Parting again, he whispered, "You're delicious."

She licked her lips and whispered, "Just one more?"

Lips met again, their tongues dancing together. Her hands slid on his back, holding him to her, and tiny moans came from her throat.

I love this, and I think I love Norman too.

He parted again and whispered, "Let's have our dinner."

"Mmm-hmm."

They sat at a table, hip to hip, alone in the park. He unwrapped the cheese first, cutting it on a small cheese board and offered her crackers, pouring wine for them. The sound of the falls was in the distance, and they could hear birds overhead. He fed her a piece of cheese on a cracker, then made one for himself.

This is so romantic. Could he be falling in love with me? Am I with him? If he's wooing me, he's doing a great job. It's happening way faster than I thought it could.

She fed him a cracker with cheese, and he kissed her fingers as she pulled back. Rising to his invitation, she touched his lips with hers, tasting the cheese on his tongue.

They sat and fed each other until the cheese was gone. Sipping their wine, they unwrapped the food, staring into each other's eyes as they ate.

What if he scraped the things from the table, lifted me and lay me on the table, then made long, slow love to me as the spray from the falls wafted over us.

He saw her eyes go distant, and he asked, "What are you thinking?"

Embarrassed, she blushed.

"The thought must have been good. Tell me."

Her eyes left his as she said, "Ummm. I imagined you making love to me, ummm, here on the table."

Pausing, as if taking her thoughts into his mind, he said, "Nothing would make me happier, on this table, the spray of the falls falling on us, but not for today. We need to talk about sex first."

Her eyes returned to his, dancing.

I'm safe for the moment. Sex, as a thought, is tantalizing, but if put into practice, it's more than a little scary, especially here, out in the open.

He said, "I'm not inexperienced with sex, and I've found out what it does to a relationship. It's so powerful that it masks what the couple has together, what they have built between them, what unites them. Their relationship, or lack of it, is exposed later when the novelty of sex wears off. Much better is to wait to be physically intimate until the relationship is on solid ground, like engaged or better, married, committed to each other fully. Then, sex is the icing on the cake, sweet, making their experience, and their lives better."

"You really think that? The pictures and text on Google seem so different."

"I have money, and many people, many women, wanted it. I had to learn not to be sucked into their ways. Those pictures and stories were from before I learned the power and danger of sex early in a relationship."

Samantha's words flooded back to her, based on what she saw and read. She was wrong about him now, as he had learned the painful lessons which changed who he was.

Christie paused, thinking, reflecting. "So, what will be the sleeping arrangements on our adventure trip?"

"I have only one room, and to get another is impossible now. But it will have two beds, so we can sleep together or apart as we want. If we sleep together, it will not be for sex. Kissing and caressing, I hope, but not sex. Are you okay with that arrangement?"

She smiled, responding, "Yeah. Sounds wonderful to me."

This is perfect. Romance and togetherness without the clouds and interpersonal glue of sex.

45

The food was finished, yet they still stared into each other's eyes, consumed by what they just talked about. After some moments, Norman blinked, and normal life returned. She collected their trash as he put the things back into the basket.

They still had a little wine left. He patted the seat next to him and said, "Come, sit next to me. We can finish our wine, watching the falls and the sunset."

Marvelous idea.

She joined him, holding her glass. Emptying the last drops into both glasses, they sat, sipping, and watching. His arm was around her, holding her to him. Birds wheeled overhead, and squirrels ran around in the trees and on the ground. They even had some squirrel fights, chasing each other around and around a tree.

Their wine finished, they put the glasses back into the basket and walked toward the car, hand in hand.

"You know, even after so short a time, I think I'm falling in love with you," said Norman.

Wow. He thinks like me. Wow. This is amazing.

Christie stopped and turned to him. "Norman, it's so good to hear you say that because I think the same thing about you. I'm falling in love with you. I never expected it to happen, but we've clicked since I first shook your hand."

Pausing for a moment, he said, "It was the spark. It must mean something to us."

"I think so."

They stood quietly, watching the sun disappear, illuminating the clouds with reds and oranges, tossing bits of cracker to squirrels, chipmunks, and birds, reflecting on what had been unveiled as they spoke.

"Are you okay to drive us home?"

"Yeah. The bottle I brought was lower in alcohol, and the time we spent here, with food, will make it okay."

She nodded, trusting his judgment, not feeling lit herself.

He drove her home as both had work in the morning. Helping her out, he walked her to her door, arm in arm. Turning to him, they kissed again, long kisses of passion. Unlocking her door, she kissed him briefly again and entered. Through the windows, she watched him get into his Roadster, that fun car, and drive away.

Running to her bedroom, she turned on a streaming station of love songs, got into the shower and sang along. Mixed in with her singing, she relived their date, moment by moment, savoring their kisses and time together.

What would it be like if Norman were in the shower with me? Would he take me? If we were married, I can't imagine him not taking me. Nothing is better than this, to have a guy in my life who's falling in love with me. And we have an adventure coming up!

Chapter 5

Norman

They loaded her suitcase and other things into Norman's Audi. "I can't believe that the day is finally here. We're off on our big adventure!" Christie exclaimed as she high-fived Norman.

Three hours into the drive, Christie worked with Maps to find a restaurant, choosing *Tracy's at Roam Inn* in Munising.

After a plate lunch, he held out the Audi fob and asked, "Do you want to drive?"

Eyes wide, "Can I?"

"Sure. It's easy, just a car. But it has lots of go, so be gentle on the accelerator."

A Star Wars fan, she got in, adjusted the seat, and prepared to commence primary ignition. Her face showed she was a little scared but got them out onto the road. No cars were in sight, so he whispered, "Punch it." The rocket ignited and roared down the road, eliciting a huge grin and a whoop from her.

"Keep it at the speed limit, though I admit, it's not easy. I use the cruise control to contain my lead foot."

"Good idea." She paused, thinking. "How fast have you gone?"

"I had it at 145 once, for a short time. No cars, straight road, it was a thrill."

She settled in and drove for an hour and a half, stopping for a break. He took over, wanting to keep their destination a secret. The address already in his GPS; in about an hour, they arrived.

She helped unload their gear, unaware of anything, thinking a boat awaited them. She saw the plane outside, a Cessna 172 on floats, tied to the dock, and Norman could see understanding come to her.

"Are we going to fly to the island in that?"

Does she want to fly or not? Don't know.

"Yeah, that's the plan. Quicker than a boat."

Leaping into the air, she exclaimed, "I've always wanted to fly a small plane but never had the chance."

He smiled at her excitement and said, "Then, you'll sit in the copilot's seat."

"Can I? For sure?" She jumped up and down from excitement. His smile showed her that he was pleased that she was so happy.

"Yeah, for sure. I'll sit in the back."

*****

Christie

Norman claimed their reservation, their pilot greeted them, they carried their luggage to the plane, and in ten minutes, they were away from the dock, engine running. Norman had told Anthony, their pilot, that Christie wanted to fly a small plane since she was little. A Cheshire-cat smile erupted on his face, and he said, "I'll give her a lesson."

"And I'll give you a tip for your services."

The smile broadened. "That would be much appreciated. Don't get many students here, not like in Alaska where they have more pilot's licenses than driver's licenses."

Anthony talked with her, gauging her abilities and interest. As he taxied them to their takeoff point, he asked, "Do you want to take her up?"

Christie's excitement ratcheted up several notches. "Can I?"

"Yeah. I'll guide you and tell you what to do. Today is calm and not tricky. You can do it."

"Oh, my. I never imagined I could do a takeoff, ever."

She focused.

"Okay. One hand on the wheel, nice and level." He rotated the wheel so she could feel it. "The other hand on the throttle, here. When I say, 'go,' push it all the way in."

Christie inhaled a deep breath and wiggled her behind in the seat. Anthony said, "Go," and she pushed the throttle in all the way. The engine roared, the plane started to move, and she whooped. Anthony had his hands on the wheel as well to steady her.

As they gathered speed, he said, "Pull back a little."

She did so, two hands on the wheel, and could feel the nose lift, though still on the water.

"Back a little more."

Suddenly gravity held them no longer, and she whooped again. She was bouncing in her seat from excitement.

"A little longer, and then we'll cut the throttle back to normal cruising power and climb to 2,500 feet," he told her, pointing to the RPM and altitude instruments.

She looked out the windows, both sides, and marveled at what she saw.

"Careful with the wheel; don't turn us quite yet."

Her attention snapped back to the front, and he helped her level the wings.

"Okay, pull the throttle back about two inches."

Pulling on it, she heard the engine slow down to 2,300 RPM.

"Do you see the compass there, above the instruments, right in the center?"

"Yes."

"Turn slightly to the right until we head due north."

Banking the wings to the right, the compass rotated.

"Straighten the wheel. Yeah. Push forward just a little. Umm-hmm. Keep the horizon line right where it is now."

She shrieked. "Norman, I'm flying. I can't believe it. I've always wanted to do this."

"Yup."

Way out in the distance, she could see the island.

Anthony said, "Turn a little to the right, head to the right of the island. We'll make a sweeping left turn around it before we land so that you can see it."

The flight was short, but in Christie's mind, it lasted forever; she absorbed every minute. As they neared the island, Anthony took over and gave them a view as he circled it, then he cut the throttle, and they glided in for a landing, giving her instructions about what he was doing the whole time. She was focused on what he said, watching the instruments and her hands softly on the wheel, with glances outside to see the water rise to greet them with thumps on the floats.

Tying up at the dock, she got out first, jumping up and down. With a huge smile on his face, Norman said, "Christie, you did it, you flew a plane. Who would have thought it?"

"Norman, you made it possible for me to achieve a dream of mine."

Norman handed their luggage out, and she grabbed the pieces, setting them on the dock. A family of four waited to take the plane back to Houghton, so they moved out of their way, but then she grabbed Norman and kissed him, saying, "Thank you so, so much for letting me fly. I've always wanted to try it."

"And you did well."

Whipping her phone out to take a picture of the plane, she insisted that Norman was in it, holding the wing strut. Anthony then volunteered to take a picture of them both, which pleased her even more.

She kissed Norman again, "If I forget to say thank you for this wonderful trip, I enjoyed it immensely; thank you so much."

Kissing her back, he whispered, "I'm glad to have you along with me. It makes the trip better. Now, it's our trip and our memory."

His words were a Cupid's arrow to her heart.

He includes me in his life, and I've always wanted that, a life partner.

A sign at the end of the dock, near some speed boats, read, "Water Taxi." Nodding toward it, pulling their cases, Norman said, "Our ride to the Lodge."

They walked toward the boats as the plane's engine started and taxied out for their takeoff. She stopped, turned, and watched until it lifted off the water and turned south, back to Houghton. Sticking her arms out like the wings of a plane, she circled Norman, her lips making engine noises until his laugh infected her, and she had to laugh as well.

"You did enjoy that plane ride."

"My year is made. And I got to fly it, too."

"If we get the same pilot, you can probably fly it back to Houghton on Monday."

That thought made her jump for joy. Norman had made a reservation for the water taxi, so they boarded and were off for a short trip to the lodge.

As they sped along, admiring the scenery, he said, "Sure beats walking."

She nodded and pointed out a moose at the edge of the lake, paying no attention to the boat. Half an hour later, they were at the Lodge desk, getting their cottage number and a map. After a short walk, they entered a cottage with a rustic look, but modern as well.

Christie said, "This is perfect. It's so fun to be here with you. Thank you so much for asking me to come along."

"To have you here with me makes it ten times more fun."

After organizing their things, they sat in their veranda chairs, enjoying the quiet of their setting.

Christie asked about the plan for the days, and Norman related his thoughts.

Quiet again, they absorbed the almost silence, letting it invade their souls. Birds flitted around their cottage, and squirrels and chipmunks scampered around the trees. Time seemed to drift by. Norman had set the alarm for six forty-five to remind them of dinner. No cell service, no Wi-Fi, but his alarms worked. Standing, they picked up their glasses and snack plate and meandered, arm in arm, to the dining room.

The meal was tasty. Christie said when they were done, "This is going to taste super tomorrow night and the next. We'll be hungry."

"For sure."

They wandered back to their cottage, hand in hand, listening to the evening sounds of the woods and the other cottage residents. Though not many people were near, the sounds of humanity, families playing, or people around a campfire filtered through the trees. The evening was cool, and they were glad they brought jackets.

In their cottage, Norman made a fire in the fireplace while Christie opened another bottle of wine. With the door and windows closed, silence, other than the crackle of the fire, reigned. Their souls grew quiet as well, invaded by the peacefulness of this place.

After many sips of their wine, Norman said, "I'll give you the double bed, and I'll take the bunk."

"Okay. Will you visit me?"

Norman nodded. "Oh yeah, wild horses couldn't keep me away from your bed," he sang, his face showing eagerness at his thought. "But as we talked about, not for sex."

I love this arrangement, romance, love, and connection without the glue of sex. This is perfect.

The wine gone, she took her pajamas into the bathroom and changed, him changing into his while they were apart.

"Are you decent?" came from behind the bathroom door.

"Waiting for you."

Emerging to find him sitting on his bed, having turned her bed down for her, he let her get in, and he got on her bed, on all fours, gazing at her body.

"Our first time in bed together," he whispered.

"Yeah, and a little scary."

"Nothing to be scared about. Nothing different from what we've already done."

He put two fingers on her naval and sauntered them slowly up her torso. After a few steps, she giggled and asked, "What are you doing?"

"Walking my way to kiss you."

Raising her head, she watched him. Taking a straight path between her breasts, his fingers strolled up her neck, with a few jumps, and did a two-finger jig on her lips, humming a tune, with her trying to grab his fingers with her lips. Her eyes danced with joy as he gazed into them. He walked up her nose, between her eyes, and into her hair, with her giggling.

No one has ever done this to me, played with me before kissing me.

As their lips touched, he moved to half-lay on her, a leg over hers, his hand caressing her.

They sank into a pool of sensuality, letting their hunger for physical connection feed on their kisses and caresses. Christie was barely awake when he rose to leave her bed for his own.

A dreamy Christie whispered, "Norman, I have to tell you, I'm not falling in love with you."

"No?"

"No. I'm already there. I need to tell you that I love you."

"Christie, my darling, I love you too."

Chapter 6

Christie

O thers chose to hike the same Mt. Ojibway trail to the lookout tower, so they visited with them from time to time. People had different hiking speeds, and Norman and Christie did not want to hurry, so often, they were alone on the trail.

They found some chipmunks as they paused for a rest. Norman had some crackers which they broke and fed them. The critters were very tame, and one even came up into Christie's hand to take the bite. Its claws tickled her palm, making her laugh. Norman took a video of their performance, and they viewed it together as they resumed their hike.

Scaling the tower, they had a grand view of almost the whole island, the Lighthouse, where they began the hike and way down to the southwest end of the island. The view was worth the hike.

Descending, they sat at one of the picnic tables for lunch. Other hikers came and went as they set their food out and ate leisurely. More chipmunks begged for bits of their lunch and were fearless in their approach. The little guys were irresistible. Also hungry were some sparrows who came in a flock when food was available. Christie had never fed wild animals before, and doing so enchanted her. Norman took videos of her as she fed them.

Lunch finished, they wandered back down the trail, meeting more hikers in a hurry to get to the tower. They were glad that time was not an issue, so they could stop to look at things along the trail. Smell the flowers on the way, as it were.

Christie's foot began to hurt, and she thought she might be getting a blister.

"I'm a wuss."

Laughing, he said, "I don't think so, only a tenderfoot."

"So true."

"I'll take a look when we get back to our cottage. Be glad we're taking the water taxi and not having to hike six more miles to the lodge."

"Oh, that's for sure. I'd never make it. You'd have to carry me."

He laughed. "So, no caveman carry, dragging you to my residence by your hair?"

Giving him an indignant look, her voice was the same. "I don't think so."

They both laughed at what he suggested and her response.

Soon, they neared the dock, happy to see the water taxi waiting for them. They walked to their cottage, tired with Christie limping a bit.

Shucking their packs inside, shaking a little to limber up, he said, smiling at her, "Okay, tenderfoot, show me those feet."

Stretching out on the bed, feet hanging over the end, sighing, she said, "It feels so good to be horizontal."

Removing her shoes and socks, she saw him wrinkle his nose and turn away.

"Oh, no, do my feet smell?"

"Nope, just kidding."

She threw a pillow at him, and he tickled the bottom of her foot, which made her giggle and pull it away.

Flipping the pillow back to her, he inspected her foot. "Yeah, you have the start of a blister, a small one. Tomorrow, wear two pairs of socks, a thin one and a thick one. Let me put a band-aid on it to cushion it for now."

Rising to find one in his pack, he returned and put it on her sore. "Tonight, I'll give you a foot massage to help you sleep."

"Oh, that would be heavenly."

Sauntering back from dinner, arm in arm, they tossed cracker pieces they saved from dinner to the chipmunks, who grabbed it, stuffed it into their pouch, asking for more.

Back in their cottage, Norman started a fire, they got into their pajamas, and they arranged the chairs so that he could give her a foot rub by the fireplace. She slid into relaxation ecstasy by the time he finished.

She whispered as he helped her to her bed, "Just make love to me and finish me off."

He laughed as she got under the covers, "Oh, how I want to, but not tonight."

Getting in with her, he whispered, "I'll be kissing you, though."

From last night, she knew what he would do and welcomed him to love on her. After a time, she rolled them, doing a two-finger walk up his torso as he did to her last night. Half-laying on him, she kissed him, caressing his chest. His hands roamed all over her back.

61

He rolled them, so she was on her back, a leg of his between hers, as they sank deeper into their pool of sensuality. After a long time, he parted, rolling onto his back next to her, caressing the back of her hand with his thumb.

As their passions cooled, she whispered, "Norman, thanks for today, and tonight. This trip is my best ever. I love you."

"My best ever too. I love you, Christie."

How fantastic is this, to have a guy who loves on me, but doesn't violate our boundaries. I can hardly wait for tomorrow.

Chapter 7

Christie

The day dawned with high clouds, portending rain. They dressed, ready for their outing once breakfast was finished. The hike was shorter and had less elevation gain. Like yesterday, they obtained a lunch from the restaurant and started out. She wore two pairs of socks, and it helped—her sore foot gave her almost no trouble.

As they walked along, they were quiet on the first part of the trail, listening to the forest sounds. Christie mused about the growing relationship she had with Norman. The pool of sensuality into which they sank in their love-times strengthened their connection.

I'm in love with this man, and it happened so fast. To be apart from him is agony, and to be with him, to play with him, just builds my desire for him. My heart is investing in him.

*****

Norman

In the quiet, Norman mused on the relationship developing between them.

The women of my past are fading into dim memories as my love for Christie grows by leaps and bounds. I enjoy being with her, listening to her, seeing her made happy, laughing by what I do, and what I offer. I can envision a life spent with her, filled with adventures and times of closeness. I want this woman—her mind, her soul, and her body.

Arriving at Lookout Louise, they found a grand view of the northern shore of the island. They sat near the water to eat their lunch. Again, chipmunks wanted a share, and Christie was eager to feed them. One took a piece of bread from her hand though nervous about the whole affair. They laughed at the chipmunk's jumpy movements, contrasted with the squirrel's smoother manner of moving.

Christie turned to Norman, her voice becoming low and seductive. "I want to feed you this apple."

She straddled his legs, sitting on his thighs, holding the apple to his teeth.

"Take a bite."

He did so, then she smeared apple juice around his mouth, slowly, intentionally, provocatively.

"Let me help you with that." Licking him, sucking on him, kissing him, cleaning him, she planted her lips on his and kissed him for a long while.

When she parted, he whispered, "I like this."

Taking the apple, he held it to her lips, saying, "Take a bite."

As she chewed, he smeared apple juice around her mouth and did as she did, cleaning her, ending with his lips on hers. The pool of sensuality had moved with them, and they sank into it, there on the shore of Lake Superior. Holding each other with their non-sticky hand, he relished their connection.

This is what I want with a woman. Christie, you make me want to lay you down on these rock slabs and make love to you. You drive me nuts.

Christie offered the core to a squirrel who grabbed it, chittered at them, and ran to a tree, climbing quickly with his prize in his mouth.

She rose from his legs, went to the water to wash, and he did the same, whispering, "You're way too much fun to be with, as well as being delicious."

"I could say the same about you."

"Norman, I need to tell you, again, that I love you."

Caressing her cheek, he said, "I love you too."

Then, he grabbed her and moved like he was going to throw her into the lake. She screamed and wrestled with him. As they struggled, their faces came together, their eyes locked, and the wrestling stopped. He held her and planted his lips on hers again, his hands in her hair, caressing her. Her arms surrounded his neck, and they clung to each other, heart investing in heart, welding themselves together.

He parted and looked at the sky, now threatening rain, saying, "We should go."

"Yeah."

About halfway back, the storm surrounded them, pelting them with rain. Starting to dance along the trail, she sang a tune, and he danced behind her. As the rain continued, branches they pushed out of their way dripped more water on them.

Skipping ahead of him, she turned, gazing into his eyes, holding a branch, threatening to release it, and shower him with rainwater.

"Don't you dare."

She had already dared, and as he neared, hand out to stop the branch, she let go. The branch hit his hand, spraying him with water. She took off, running down the trail, screaming as he chased her. He caught her, turned her to face him, and said, "You naughty girl. I'm going to punish you now."

"You are—are you?"

"Yeah." With that, he planted his lips on hers and pulled her body to his, kissing her with passion.

When he parted, she whispered, "I like this punishment. May I have another, sir?"

He obliged her, and they kissed for a long time with rain falling on them. Fortunately, their cottage was not far, as they were soaked when they arrived, dripping on the floor as they walked in. He said, "Go take a hot shower and warm up. I'll start a fire and then do the same when you finish."

"Okay."

Norman had the fire blazing when Christie emerged, wrapped in a towel that covered only her essentials. He wiped his brow of the sweat forming, not because of the fire. He locked eyes with her, his hunger for her growing.

Christie, how I want that towel to slip, or better yet, I want to remove it from you, slowly, carry you to bed and make love to you. Woman, you drive me insane.

The oh-so pregnant moment passed, and she whispered innocently, "I forgot my dry clothes."

"So, I see."

Choosing an outfit, moving carefully not to let her towel slip or bend over, she retreated into the bathroom to change. She emerged, carrying her wet things and said, "Your turn."

Raising his eyebrows, he said, "You look good in that outfit, but you, in only a towel, are a definite attraction."

She slapped his arm as he passed, saying, "I should hope so."

Learning from her, he took his dry clothes in with him. Having hung her wet things on chairs to dry, she sat by the fire.

*****

Christie

Staring into the flames, Christie reflected on their relationship.

If we had no agreement between us, I would have dropped my towel and let him take me, or even emerged without a towel, or even better, invited him into the shower with me. I've seen him want me, hungry to take me. What would it be like to let it happen? Is he a good lover?

She shook herself to rid her mind of those thoughts, shifting to what she liked about him. Thoughts filled her mind as he emerged, sitting beside her, enjoying the warmth of the fire.

Quiet surrounded them, staring at the burning logs and dancing flames. She said, "You know, these three days have been the best of my life."

"I'd say the same. I've never been with a woman like you; to play with, to talk with, to be together, and enjoy every minute."

"Norman, I've said it before, but I need to say it again. I love you."

"I love you too. I truly think you are the woman for me, for my whole life."

Staring into the flames, they reflected on their words, words of commitment to each other. After some long moments, hand in hand, he pulled her to sit on his lap, like she did feeding him the apple. They kissed, pressed together, saying, "I love you," when they parted, alternating until his phone dinged for dinner.

The rain stopped as they emerged from the lodge after dinner, so they strolled back to their cottage, listening to the drops from the trees hit the ground. The quiet was more intense as the rain had driven the people into their cabins. Their cabin welcomed them, the fire still burning but low. Norman added a couple of logs, and it brightened, filling the room with its dancing light.

He asked, "Do you want wine?"

"No. I'm good for now."

They sat for a while longer, and he said, "We should get some sleep. The plane comes for us at ten."

Both of them knew what would happen next. For two nights, she wore full pajamas, but tonight she emerged in a close-fitting T-shirt and skimpy sleep shorts. He sat up in bed and whistled at her, pulling her covers down. As she got into bed, he whispered, "That's a provocative look for you."

"I wanted to give you something to look at and not be bored," she murmured, running her hands up her sides tantalizingly.

"Goal accomplished. I'm never bored with you."

Part of her was glad for their agreement, reasonably confident that he would hold to it, but the other part, the I-need-him part, wanted him to take her, to be sensuously undressed and even more

68

sensuously made love to. She was confident that he knew what to do in that department.

He got in with her and moved toward her, gazing at her with eyes of hunger. Her imagination soared with memories of their love-times. They sank into their pool of sensuality, as he spoke love-words to her, kissed her, and caressed her; the pleasure from their physical connection and her imagination carried her toward the peaks of ecstasy.

Norman, you make me want to rip my clothes off and throw myself at you. Nothing is better than this, to be in love and have my man next to me, loving on me, telling me that he loves me.

Chapter 8

Christie

They woke with her half-laying on him, snuggled into him, her leg over his, her arm across his middle, and her head resting on his arm.

I love this. I love him. Only being married could be better.

He was warm, and she caressed his chest, touching him, sniffing his scent of man and lingering perfume, feeling of him, his skin, his hair, his muscles. His hand was on her back, doing the same thing. Neither wanted to rise from this comfy position. Moving to kiss him, they connected for long moments.

When she parted, he said, "We should get up and prepare for the day. We both have work tomorrow and miles to go before we sleep."

A sad, "I know," came from her mouth.

As she stood, she said, "We slept together all night."

He grinned, running his hands through his hair. "And, without sex."

"But with some fantastic make-out time. It's amazing our boundaries held."

Not that I didn't want him to make love to me, just not today.

In the water taxi by 9:30, they could see and hear their plane arriving as they neared the Lighthouse dock. Waiting on the dock as the plane taxied to a stop, they watched Anthony hop out to tie up.

Turning to Christie, he asked, "Do you want to fly us back?"

"Do birds have feathers?"

Laughing, he helped Norman load their luggage. Soon, they taxied back out onto the lake.

Anthony said, "Let me take off, as it's a little tricky with the waves still present from the storm. But then I'll give her to you to fly us home."

Her excitement mounted as she watched what he did. Soon they were at full power, bouncing on the waves, struggling to defeat the pull of gravity. One last bounce and they were airborne. A few hundred feet up, Anthony said, "She's all yours."

Christie gripped the wheel as he said, "Crank us around to the right to a course of 180, slowly."

"Mmm-hmm," came her reply, as she dipped the wings.

"Pull back on the wheel a little as you turn, to keep us climbing."

"Yup," she commented as she watched the compass. At 180, she leveled the wings, bouncing in her seat a little from excitement.

Showing her the altimeter, he said, "When we get to 2,500 feet, we'll stop climbing." He showed her the rate-of-climb indicator and showed her how pulling or pushing on the wheel affected it. Looking outside, shifting her eyes inside, checking the instruments, and then repeating her visual path consumed her. Yet, her heart soared like an eagle's.

When they could see Houghton in the distance, he took over, praising her in her second flying lesson. She glowed. Anthony landed and tied up at the dock. Christie climbed out, and Norman handed her the luggage. To Anthony, he handed a sizable cash tip for two flying lessons, and they made their way to the car, a rocket-ship of its own, and a lot quieter than the Cessna.

Stowing their things in the trunk, they started out. After some minutes, Norman said, "By the way, I had a text from my father, inviting us to New York for Thanksgiving for the five-day weekend. Would you like to go?"

"Wow, meet the parent. This is serious now."

"Dad's a nice guy. He's all business at work, but he was a fun father. He left work at work, and he was always with mom and me when he was home. It'll be fun."

"Okay. My schedule is always so full, but I'll make time."

He laughed, and so did she.

"I'll tell him, and he'll send the jet."

Christie turned to him, paused for a moment and exclaimed, "He'll send the jet?"

"Yeah, his company has a jet contract, and they need to spend the hours. So, he'll send the jet, take us to New York, and then bring us back."

"Seriously? We'll fly to New York in a private jet?"

"Yeah. What's the problem?"

"Never, in a million years, would I envision myself flying in a private jet."

"You just flew a Cessna 172 floatplane. A jet is not much different, just more comfortable and a lot faster. What's the problem?"

We're so different economically. He just spent a bunch of money on me. I could never afford to take that trip, ever. To him, it's nothing. To me, it's unattainable. Can we really be together with this difference between us? I don't know.

She chose to abdicate and said, "Not a problem."

*****

Norman

Silence filled the car until Christie asked, "Do you like my body?"

Norman knew that there was only one possible answer to that question. "Yes, I love your body. You're expressive, and your clothes give you a feminine look that's very enjoyable to me."

He paused to see how that would go. Fortunately, it was the truth. Then he added, "Why do you ask?"

I know women. The real question is at least two questions away.

Christie paused for a long moment. Glancing at her, she was serious, thinking, forming an answer.

"Well, you don't touch me, except to kiss me or hold me."

I bet her love-language is touch, and after our cuddling, she wants more, to go further, for me to arouse her. I can't do that, because I can't finish what we'd start. Our boundaries would shatter.

"If I did touch you that way, to arouse you, I'd make love to you. I'm trying to hold to our agreement."

"Oh."

Pausing for her to think, he said, "Is there something else that made you ask that question?"

"I've seen pictures of the women you dated before, and they were curvy, much more so than me. I'm not like them."

Now, we're getting there, to her fears. Her mind must be churning with this.

"Most of those women chased me, usually for my money. Rarely did I choose them, which is why I'm not with them now. They didn't want me; rather, they wanted my status or money."

More silence passed as she reflected on his words.

Her fears are still not coming out.

"Christie, what are you really thinking? Tell me so I can understand."

"Ummm. Okay. Ummm."

Pausing before blurting out, "My boobs are small and ummm, my hips are too. I was flat as a board until, ummm, I was fifteen. And everyone, the mean girls especially, called me pencil when I was a teen."

The real problem just emerged.

"What a terrible thing to say to you. You're definitely not that now, you are all woman and I love your body."

A long pause. "Ummm. But, ummm, my boobs are small."

"But I bet they're sensitive, and if caressed, would cause your body to soar toward ecstasy? Want to test them out once we get home?"

She giggled and blushed at his words. Shyly she said, "But, we have an agreement that doesn't allow that."

"True, but agreements can be broken."

"Ummm. They can be, but that, ummm, would lead to more, ummm—"

"Yes. And, unless you want me to stop the car, to test out your body right now, to show you how beautiful you are and how well you'll respond to being touched, we should probably change the subject."

Laughing this time, she said, "Good idea. We might need to turn up the air to cool us down."

I'm glad her fear is out.

"Maybe."

Silence filled the car.

After a time, she offered, "Thanks for letting me talk about that." She paused, thinking. "So, tell me about your parents."

"Better subject. Mom died of cancer about ten years ago, and her death crushed my father, though he recovered over time. It was the same for me. We were a very close, fun family. My father was there for us when he was not working."

"So sorry for your loss, that must have been hard, being close."

"It was, but not so much now. Mom is a memory, a good one, but a memory. What about your parents?"

"They're both gone." Her voice sounded strained, and the silence became very thick for a moment.

Hesitating, he asked, "How did they die?

Regarding her, he saw her face wrinkle. "I've never told anyone about it."

"You don't have to tell me now."

Her shoulders shrugged, and her eyes looked to her feet. "I probably should, so you know everything about me."

"You can wait if you want."

"I want to tell you, to get it out and unload what I've been carrying for all these years."

His hand moved to her thigh, caressing her to her knee, comforting her.

"Okay."

Silence filled the car as a glass fills with water from a pitcher before it can overflow.

Inhaling a deep breath, pausing, she said, "My father murdered my mother and then killed himself." She exhaled a sharp breath. "There, I told you."

He turned to her, his eyebrows raised in surprise, but saw relief in her eyes.

"What? Really? Why? How?"

"He would get high on something. I was little and didn't know what, but he would call her the devil, and they would fight, verbally, and physically. Ummm. She defended herself, I saw it. That night, ummm, he was high, had a gun from somewhere and shot her, five times, then himself once."

Her hands slapped her thighs as a finale.

"And you were there?"

Nodding, pausing, thinking, she shivered to remember the event. "The gunfire woke Jimmy and me. We went in and saw the bodies, collapsed, bleeding all over. I went into shock, but Jimmy called 911."

"How awful."

"The police came and took us away before they took our parent's bodies. Fortunately, Dad actually set up a trust for us. He was pretty smart when he wasn't a druggie. It owned the house where James lives and the house in Petoskey."

"That's terrible. So, do you feel better, now that you told me?"

"Yeah. Whew. My secret is out now, and it's like a load lifted from me."

"I'd think so."

"Do you think I'm terrible? I've not done anything with myself other than a two-year associate's degree."

"How could I feel that way? Your childhood was horrid, and you had no one to help you or encourage you. You're doing great for such a difficult background."

"You really think so?"

"Yes."

He could see and sense her relax with his acceptance of her as she was, despite their differences.

*****

Christie

They talked about New York for a long time, what it was like as a kid, and then what it was like when he was in college. The picture Norman portrayed was a magical one to Christie.

She had seen the Macy's Parade on TV, but to see it up close, and to fly there on a private jet was beyond what she could imagine. The more she thought about it, rolling the possibilities around in her mind, the more excited she became.

As they neared Petoskey, Christie spoke in an almost shy voice, "Could we spend one more night together before reality envelopes us?"

"Absolutely, and I need to text my father to tell him that we're coming. Does the schedule we talked about work for you?"

Her voice changed to almost indignant, nose in the air. "You know my schedule is always full. I may have to move some things."

He laughed at her ways.

Still indignant, "Why are you laughing. Don't you know I'm a social butterfly, and I flit everywhere all the time." Her hands made tiny flitting movements at her shoulders, and she started to giggle, not able to hold her haughty attitude together.

*****

Christie

Christie changed into a tight, short T-shirt and sleep shorts in the bathroom, as he changed in the bedroom, and he pulled the covers down for her. She emerged, and they regarded each other, knowing what had transpired in bed at the lodge, but something seemed different now that they would be together in his bed.

Letting her get in, he turned to her with eyes of a lion regarding a gazelle. "So, shall we play boobies, to see if they'll send messages all through your body?"

An indignant look crossed her face as she said, "No. Our agreement is still in place."

They regarded each other, and her face changed to one of embarrassed desire, "Well, maybe just a little, so I can feel what it's like, with you."

"Clothes on?" he asked as his smile broadened.

"Yes, clothes on."

Already, the bumps on her shirt grew in her anticipation. The chase was a familiar one.

Starting at her bare navel, he did a slow, sensual, four-fingered walk up her body, traversing back and forth. She alternately giggled or moaned as her body responded. He meandered between her breasts and then around each one, in a figure-eight. Her tight buds had grown as he caressed her, now being pronounced bumps under her shirt.

"Grab onto the headboard."

She felt the decorative wrought iron frame and found a grip, lifting her breasts to form perfect hills. From between her breasts, he chose to circle her left breast and began a spiral caress-walk to the top.

He whispered, "How does that feel?"

A passion-filled voice said, "Oh, my, it feels wonderful. You're sending messages everywhere, even to my toes."

As he neared her nipple, now tall under her shirt, he let his fingers graze it, one after the other, a gasp coming from her throat as he did so. He made his last circle and let his fingers surround her nipple, closing on it, lifting it, and turning it. Pleasure caused Christie to pant, arch her back, pushing her breast into his fingers, moaning and cooing at him. After some long moments of caressing her, he spiraled down to her chest and then up her right breast, eliciting panting, more sounds, and body motions from her.

After caressing her right nipple, he spiraled down to her chest, meandered up her neck to her lips, did a four-fingered jig there which made her giggle, then wandered into her hair as his lips closed on hers.

A moan and "Oh my," escaped from her mouth as he parted from their kiss. After a time, he whispered, "So, what do you think of your boobs now? Does size limit sensitivity?"

Dreamy eyes opened to his, and her bottom lip disappeared between her teeth. "Mmmmmmmmmmm." She whispered, "Ummm, ummm, no. They seem pretty sensitive, and you made me feel wonderful. They sent messages everywhere. Ummm, you could keep that up for a while if you want." Her eyes drifted closed, then opened and stared dreamily into his.

Kissing her, he whispered, "And, if I did, you'd be nude, and our agreement would be broken within seconds."

A bit less dreamy, she added, "Probably true, and I'd want that to happen, but not right now, as I'm glad we have our agreement."

"Me too."

After a pause and more caresses, he said, "Roll over, so I can snuggle with you and let us sleep," he whispered.

"Norman, I love you. Thanks for taking me on our trip."

"Christie, I love you too, and you being with me made it way more fun."

Part-Time Worker, Full-Time Lover

Chapter 9

Christie

Wednesday before Thanksgiving came within moments, it seemed. Christie would go to dinner at his house from three to five times a week, and she would sleepover with him, though they kept to their agreement. One sensitivity test of her breasts was enough for her to know how marvelous sex would be with Norman. He knew what to do, and he convinced her that her body would respond to him.

On the travel day, he picked her up at eleven, putting her suitcase in the back, taking her to his house until they had to leave for the airport.

The drive to the Petoskey airport was short, and a gleaming, silver plane sat on the tarmac, three uniformed people standing at the entryway, smiling.

"Is that ours?"

"Yeah. The pilots are Tom and Theodore, and the flight attendant is Joan. They're all wonderful people, very professional, and I enjoy the flight when they're our crew."

Walking toward the plane, arm in arm, they pulled their cases behind them. Tom said as they neared them, "Norman, it's so nice to see you again." Theodore and Joan nodded.

"And who is this beautiful lady?"

Christie blushed, and her eyes went to the tarmac. Norman looked at Christie as he said, "This is my extra-special girlfriend, Christie. We flew to Isle Royale for a few days, and our pilot gave her a couple of impromptu flying lessons. I'm sure she would love to see your flight deck."

Christie inhaled sharply, a huge smile erupted on her face, like that of the Cheshire Cat.

Tom looked at her and said, "By her smile, I'll take that as an agreement to your suggestion."

Theodore took their suitcases; Tom held his arm out to Christie as he said, "Come with me, you pilot in training."

She stammered, "Okay."

Norman shook Theodore's hand and mouthed, "Thank you." Joan grinned. Once Christie and Tom climbed aboard, they joined them.

Christie and Tom entered the flight deck. He said to her, "You sit in the left seat, the captain's seat. I'll be your copilot."

She wormed her way in and sat. She had been amazed by the Cessna's instruments. This was beyond her imagination. Everything glowed, orange, green or red, and instruments or controls were above her, below her, covering all the space she could reach.

Tom said, "It's basically the same as a Cessna 172, but we have two engines, so there are two throttles. We have fancier radios, more instruments, display screens with lots of info, and other navigation aids, but flying is flying. With some instruction, you could do it."

Showing her the instruments she knew, he explained others, grouped in clusters. Her mind whirled with all that he said. "Once we get airborne, Joan will let you come up to see what we do."

"Oh, that would be wonderful."

Getting out of the seat, she moved back to the main cabin. Norman sat already, facing aft, with a table between him and her chair. A sofa was across from them. Her eyes were as big as saucers as she sat, saying to Norman, "That was so cool. Tom said I could come back once we're airborne."

"I'm glad."

Joan came to them, advising them to fasten their seat belts and gave them emergency instructions. Afterward, she moved forward and knocked on the cockpit door. Moments later, the engines started, and within five minutes, they were airborne. Once the seat belt sign went dark, Joan came to Christie and asked, "Want to see the cockpit in action?"

"Sure."

Joan knocked on the door, and Theodore opened it, inviting Christie in, showing her the jump-seat. She was with them for half an hour and returned with huge eyes, bouncing on her toes.

"They showed me everything. It was so cool."

Clapping his hands joyously, smiling broadly, he said, "I'm glad you could see them in action."

Sitting, her eyes went distant. As he regarded her, it was as if he could see the wheels in her mind spinning, and he smiled at being able to please her.

"Tom said that we would fly into Teterboro Airport, the one where Sully was directed to land but didn't have the altitude to make it."

Norman nodded, saying, "I remember from his book."

Joan came, asking if they wanted a snack and a drink.

Norman asked Christie, "Wine?"

She nodded, and Norman said, "Sweet white if you have it, for me too."

Joan brought two small bottles of Riesling, cups, and sandwiches. They clinked plastic cups as he said, "Here's to our New York adventure."

Talking about their adventure as they ate and drank, Joan brought them a second bottle.

After landing, Christie bear-hugged both Tom and Theodore as they exited, thanking them for her time on their flight deck. Norman thanked them for a good flight and said, "See you on Sunday."

"We'll be here for you," Tom assured.

A limo waited for them as they deplaned. The driver stowed their cases in the back as Norman helped Christie into the vehicle. She whispered, "There's room for ten people in here. Who else is joining us?"

Norman laughed. "Just us."

Her eyes got wide. The disparity of their economic situation showed up again in her heart. But, she repelled it with, *I could get used to this. Oh, yeah.*

"Sit back and relax. It's about a 45-minute drive to Dad's building."

Christie moved from seat to seat, looking at everything as they neared the city, making Norman laugh, though he pointed out sights as they passed them. Winding their way through the city, they arrived at Dad's apartment building. A doorman opened their door, and the driver handed them their cases. Christie was rubber-necked, looking at everything. Norman had her arm in his, or she would have fallen over. He moved them toward the door, which the doorman opened for them, then to the elevator to the 28th floor and his father's apartment. Norman rang the bell, and soon a man appeared in the doorway, smiling, with bright eyes.

"Junior, it's so good to see you," the older man said as they shook hands, and then his dad surrounded him in a big hug.

Turning to Christie, he said, "And, you must be Christie."

She stared into his eyes, warm eyes for her.

"Come here, young lady, let me hug you."

"Mr. Peale, it's so nice to meet you."

"Call me Norman, please, or better, Dad."

Christie's mind expected a stuffy banker who might have shaken her hand, but to have him hug her and have her call him, Dad, was way outside of the box.

He held her tightly and more prolonged than was expected for a first meeting. Letting her go, he said, "It's so nice to meet you. Junior says wonderful things about you, and now that I see you, I'm sure they're all true. Come in, please. Take your things to your room. Ummm. I presume that you're together in one room?"

"Yes, Dad, we are," said Junior.

"Okay."

Leading the way to their room, Dad said, "Change into something comfortable. I have dinner reservations for us at seven. The attire there is business casual."

Christie took in the elegant furnishings and the more than outstanding view of Central Park as she walked. Their room was large with a king bed and similarly beautiful furnishings. Christie had to work to keep her mouth closed from awe. With the door closed, Christie said, "I was not expecting him to be so warm and friendly."

"Well, he is. And, he was a wonderful father as I grew up."

She took some jeans and a top into the bathroom to change, while Norman changed in the bedroom. Emerging from their room, Dad asked, "Would you like some wine and snacks?"

Christie said, "Sure."

"Sweet white, a Riesling, as I remember Junior telling me."

"Yes, that would be wonderful."

"I have a tasty Gewürztraminer."

"Wonderful," she replied, looking at Norman, as she didn't know the name.

"You'll love it."

Retiring to the living room, Dad brought the bottle and three glasses on a silver tray and went back into the kitchen.

Junior opened the wine and poured. Dad appeared with another silver tray of scrumptious looking canapes. She had never seen such gorgeous appetizers. Turning to Dad, she asked, "Did you make these?"

He laughed and said, "Oh, no. My chef, Arthur, who will make our Thanksgiving dinner on Friday, made them, knowing you'd be here today."

Christie took one, careful not to tilt it to have something fall off. Popping it into her mouth, she hummed in approval. Once she chewed, she said, "This was scrumptious. No, way better than that. It was fantastic."

Dad laughed, saying, "I'm glad you like them. I do too."

Dad asked, "So, Christie, I've heard Junior's version of how you met. Tell me your side."

Smiling at both Norman and Dad, with Norman taking her hand, she said, "It's pretty simple. Norman hired me as a temp worker when all of his assistants were out with the flu. When I shook his hand on the first day, we had a spark that drew our eyes together. The next day, I tested it again, shaking his hand and *zap*, there was the spark again. Then on Friday, when we were done, he asked me to dinner, and now, here we are." Her hands went into the air, palms up, and her head tilted as if the answer was obvious.

Dad said, "How marvelous. I had a spark between my wife, Maggie, and me when we first met, and we had a wonderful life together. She died some years ago, and it took me a while to get past it. She meant the world to me."

Christie could see his eyes water and heard a crack in his voice.

Her death is still close to the surface of his emotions.

To change the subject, she said, "Could you point out the landmarks that you can see from your windows. The view is marvelous."

As if thankful for her sensitivity, he took her to the window and pointed out various things that could be seen, which she might know about. She nodded as she recognized them. Dad's hand was on her back, connecting with her, standing close to her.

The wine and snacks gone, Dad asked, "Would you like a rest before dinner. We should leave at six-thirty."

"Yeah, that would be helpful," said Junior.

They rose and sauntered toward their room. Once out of Dad's sight, she scampered for their room with him in hot pursuit, trying to pinch her behind. She ran into their room, turned and launched herself at him, webbing him in legs and arms with her lips on his. Parting, she whispered, "Thanks for bringing me here. Your Dad is just wonderful. I love him already."

Letting her down, he whispered, "I can see that he loves you already too."

"But, more importantly, I love you, Norman."

"And, my darling Christie, I love you so much."

He picked her up with her squeaking, set her on the bed, and joined her as she scooted over. He lay half on her, a leg over hers, and kissed her, his hand caressing her ear, buried in her hair.

My man loves me; he tells me that he does, and he kisses me like he does. The last thing is to have him make love to me like he does. We're almost there. Boundaries are made to be broken!

Chapter 10

Christie

A limo, like before, but with a different driver, waited at the curb and whisked them to a restaurant. Dad commented to Christie, "You look wonderful tonight. I'm so happy to take you two out."

Softly kissing her cheek not to muss her makeup, Junior added, "I think she's gorgeous, the most beautiful girl in the world."

Her response was, looking down, "You guys make me blush."

Norman whispered into her ear, "It's true."

They entered a dimly lit, romantic establishment where the host greeted them with, "Mr. Peale. It's so nice to see you tonight. Norman, it's nice to see you too. And, is this your wife?"

Christie giggled, saying, "Not a wife yet, but hope springs eternal."

Dad touched her arm and said, "Good answer."

The host led them to a table with a view of the kitchen, Dad commenting that it was his favorite table. She could see fire erupt in front of one of the chefs, over his head. The menu was extensive and made her mouth water. Dad ordered some appetizers to share, they chose an entrée, and a dessert cart would come by later.

Dad talked about his business, and Christie asked him questions about it, being so foreign to her. He dealt with billions, and she dealt with a hundred. They talked about the parade tomorrow. The box offered front row seats above the crowd with some heaters to keep them warm. Clear weather, but cold, was the forecast, in the 40s at parade time. The meal was superb, though none had room for dessert despite the temptations.

The limo picked them up, whisking them back to Dad's apartment and bed. Christie changed into shorts and a tight T, with Norman nodding in approval. Joining her in bed, her desire overcame her reason, causing her to ask in a soft, shy voice, "Could we play, ummm, boobies, ummm, like we did the other night?"

Pausing for a moment, smiling, he said, "So, that felt good to you?"

"Oh, you have no idea how marvelous it felt."

Turning to him, she saw his eyes of hunger.

"Clothes on, or off?"

Not ready to disrobe for him, but with her desire pushing her, she compromised, "How about under my top?"

Her tight buds already pushed on her shirt. "Okay. Relax and let me love on you."

He began as he did, kissing her with his hand brushing her ear, moving all around it, buried in her hair, caressing her, speaking soft words of love to her. The anticipation of his attention caused her to begin to pant as pleasure rolled through her in waves. The headboard was a wrought iron design, and he whispered, "Grab hold of the headboard."

Her hands went back, feeling of the iron until she found a hold, which lifted her breasts to perfect mounds on her chest, peaked by her nipples. His hand left her ear and slid under her T, slowly caressing her breasts, one, then the other, letting her stiff buds flip through his fingers. Waves of pleasure flowed through her, her head sank back into the pillow, and she moaned from an open mouth as she panted. He caressed her whole breast, one, then the other, lifting, playing with her nipples. Her hips began to rotate just a little, involuntary motion from her pleasure. He flew her upward until she leveled, he kept her there for a time with his caresses, then his hand went back into her hair, and he parted his kisses, laying on his back at her side, letting her float back to earth.

"So, how was that?"

Still a little breathless, she whispered back, "Oh, it was marvelous. I floated way above the earth, somewhere in the clouds, light and fluffy. I was ready for you to keep going and make love to me."

"I'm glad that I could pleasure you, even if we didn't make love."

"Oh, you did pleasure me. You really did, but I'm so sleepy."

"Not unexpected." He whispered, "Lay on me and go to sleep, my darling."

She got out, "I love you," before she drifted off.

"I love you too."

*****

Norman

The morning dawned, with Norman waking before Christie, with her laying half on him, her arm across his chest, warm and snuggled into him. He mused on their relationship, without sex in the beginning, last night halfway there.

I love that I can arouse her and make her feel fantastic. I'm pleasured when she is. I love this woman more and more each day. Is she bothered by our economic differences? This is her first interaction with old money and its people. How will it go?

Christie stirred, clutching him, but remained asleep.

I wonder if Cybill Maybree will be there, my old nemesis. She's so fake, heart, body, and speech. I need to warn Christie about her, for her to not be bothered if Cybill kisses me or fabricates some slimy verbal nonsense.

They prepared for the parade. Norman sat her on the bed, sitting next to her, his arm around her. "I need to tell you about today. Some of the women who might be there were old girlfriends or wanna-be girlfriends of mine before I left New York for Petoskey."

"Yeah? Old girlfriends?"

Norman nodded. "Some of them never understood why I left, both the city and them. They're social climbers, snakes, always looking for an in, thinking I might still be attracted to them. I follow them on Facebook, mostly to see what they're up to, you know—keep your friends close, your enemies closer."

"My, they sound terrible."

"They have conniving minds encased in beautiful womanly bodies. They know how to manipulate men into getting what they want."

"Thanks for warning me."

He touched her between her breasts, over her heart. "You are my woman, the love of my life. My heart is tied to you. Be confident in that."

Christie, staring into his eyes, nodded.

*****

Christie

A limo took them to their box at about ten. Already canapés, wines, soft drinks, and champagne were on tables behind them. Christie clung to Junior as Dad showed them where they would sit. She surveyed the women. Their high-end, red-soled shoes, clothes, and jewelry from Tiffany's or higher made her feel that her things came from the Dollar Store. She felt way out of place here. Yet, Dad made her feel at home, surrounded by this extreme luxury as best he could. He waited on her with food and drinks as the parade began.

A strikingly beautiful woman worked her way through the people, her eyes fastened on Norman. He whispered in Christie's ear, "Here comes Cybill. Get ready."

The woman wore a slinky, red, low-cut dress, displaying cleavage from her more than ample assets. Once out of the crowd, she runway walked toward Norman, making her body sway seductively. Christie wanted to vomit.

Arms out, she approached Norman, throwing them around his neck, kissing his mouth passionately, lingering on his lips as if trying to convince him that he needed her. Parting, she said, "It's so good to see you, after all this time. You need to move back to New York, away from that dirt-road village you live in. Savages are encamped right outside, yes?"

Norman did not put his arms around her, just held them out, waiting for her to release him.

She parted and backed away just a little, scanning Christie with eyes of utter disdain. "And who is this, your tart of the week? Norman, you need to come back here, to the real women, away from those earthy, native girls."

Christie's stomach churned as Norman backed away, putting his arm around Christie, hugging her to him. Her hands balled into fists, ready to punch Cybill's lights out.

Suddenly Dad appeared out of nowhere. "Cybill, it's so nice to see you again. Here, come with me, so I can get you a glass of bubbly." He steered her toward the champagne, away from Junior and Christie, with his arm around her waist.

With her turned away, Christie relaxed and whispered to Norman, "Whew. You were right; she's a snake. Dad rescued us."

Nodding, he hugged her again, planting a silent kiss on her ear, saying, "Yeah. Dad can spot a fake a mile away. Ignore her and anything she said."

The parade began, the first huge balloons appearing down the street, wrangled by handlers on ropes. Christie and Norman took their seats, soon joined by Dad.

She had imagined what the parade would be like, but this was way beyond what she had thought. The balloons were so up close and personal. They could see everything, close enough to touch them, it seemed. Each balloon seemed to surpass the previous one. She was in awe of what the parade designers had accomplished.

After an hour, the food changed to entrées in chafing dishes, beef, fish, chicken, pasta, sides, full meals of delicious offerings. Christie wanted some of everything, just to taste it all. Later, it all changed again to desserts, a plethora of temptations, but she could not eat another thing until the end, when she sneaked a couple of fruit tarts, out of this world in flavor.

The parade ended, and Dad suggested they wait a bit until the crowds dispersed, so the limo could get to them easier. Christie sampled another dessert while they waited. Thirty minutes made a difference, and the limo was close. They were whisked back to Dad's apartment, reliving the parade, looking at her pictures on her phone, though she was so close that the whole balloon was not in the frame unless it was way up the street.

*****

Christie

The afternoon flowed by, dinner came and went, and it was time for bed. When they were alone, Christie shyly asked, "Can we play boobies again tonight?"

"So, you liked that last night."

"Oh, my, yes."

"Okay, but only if I can put my mouth on you. You already know what my fingers can do."

Her eyes widened, and she giggled in anticipation. "Okay."

"Grab on."

Her hands went to the headboard, and he began to kiss her. Tonight, he kissed her, starting on her lips, then down her neck. When he would part, he would whisper love words to her, "I love you," "You're gorgeous," "You're the woman for me," and more. As he uncovered her breasts, he began to kiss around them, slowly moving uphill on one breast, his fingers doing the same on her other side. By the time he latched onto her nipple, she was panting, head back, mouth open, flying in the stratosphere. Her legs rubbed on each other involuntarily. She rose and rose and rose until her legs clamped together, a big sigh came from her, and she melted in release.

He whispered, a huge smile on his face, "Bingo."

He pulled her shirt back down, gave her breasts a gentle caress, touching her lips as he rolled to his back. She rolled onto him, a leg over his, asleep within seconds.

Deep in the night, she woke from a dream, a nightmare where the women of the box, Cybill as their leader, in their high priced goods and artificial bodies belittled her, one after another, until she was the size of an ant in their eyes. She woke with a start, stabbed in the heart by those women, remembering Samantha's words of him using her and throwing her away.

*****

Christie

Friday dawned clear again. Christie and Norman slept in until a little after nine, coming out to get coffee in robes with her clinging to him. Dad regarded them as if he knew what happened that night.

He must know what we're doing. His own times with his wife would be a memory, a good one, but sad that she's gone.

Dad told them that Arthur would arrive at about noon, and they would eat about four. Christie was excited to watch him, a real chef in action. They went back in to shower and change into comfy

99

clothes for the day. The dream was still fresh in her mind, Cybill's face morphing to an evil hag, but she said nothing about it.

Arthur arrived on time with a cart of goods. Christie helped him unpack and asked, "Where's the bird?"

"Oh, that's a secret I learned years ago. Cook it the day before. Carve it when it's cool, much easier, and gives a better product. Then all the mess can be disposed of. Cover the slices with the juices, then when they're heated, the aroma is still there, just not the mess."

"Good to know."

He began making canapés, and she watched him, taking pictures. They came out wonderfully, a variety of bases and toppings. Dad offered glasses of the Gewürztraminer from yesterday, offering to Arthur as well. The four of them drank wine and ate canapés, talking about the parade more. Arthur listened and commented on his view from TV as he prepped for today. The difference was interesting to Christie.

He limited the number of canapés to not ruin their hunger for his main meal. Commencing at two, he organized the dishes, timing them, so they would all be done about the same time. Both ovens and all the burners in use, then voila, just before four, it was all ready. He set it out on the island, everyone took a plate, including Arthur, filled them and proceeded to eat. Christie said to him, "This is the best, most elegant Thanksgiving meal I've ever eaten."

Dad and Norman echoed her sentiments, making Arthur take a bow for them. Wine flowed freely, and everyone was happy, enjoying their food and fellowship. Halfway through dinner, Arthur put apple and pumpkin pies into a slow oven to heat them gently, to preserve the crust.

Dessert was eaten on the sofa, looking out over Central Park. Arthur offered an extra sharp Vermont white cheddar with the apple pie, which Christie had never tried. She thought it fantastic, a bite of pie and cheese together was such a perfect combination of flavors.

The day wound down. Arthur cleaned up, Christie and Norman helped, him at the sink, her at the dishwasher, and Arthur packaging the leftover food. In moments the kitchen sparkled once again. Dad insisted that Arthur take some for himself, and he graciously accepted, exiting to be with his family.

Conversation with more wine flowed into the evening until bedtime.

As they sauntered to their room, he patted her behind. He smiled at her and whispered, "Play boobies tonight?"

Turning to him, with pleading eyes, she said, "I can't—not tonight. I had a climax last night, a small one. If that happens again, I'll want more, I'll want everything, and our agreement will be broken. I don't want that for us, not right now."

The images from her dream haunted her. She couldn't voice them, but they sounded in her mind over and over.

"Then, I'll just kiss you and hold you tonight. I understand your thinking and agree to hold our agreement together."

You don't understand my thinking, only part of it, but I can't tell you the rest, not now, not while we're in New York.

An inner sadness crept into her, slowly filling her as a pitcher pours water into a glass.

They met in bed, he kissed her and spooned with her.

Deep in the night, a new dream haunted her, similar to the first, except this time, the women had knives, long machetes, and chopped

101

her apart, piece by piece. Cybill was the most eager with her eyes of evil and the longest blade. Waking with a start, breathing frantically, she looked around, but it was only a dream.

*****

Christie

Saturday was to be a fun day. Christie's second dream haunted her more than the first, but she determined to push it away. At breakfast, they made a plan to see the sights in the city.

Christie wanted a subway ride, so the three of them eschewed the limo, walking through the thronging masses to the subway station. Norman handed her a token, with a hole in the middle, which she turned over and over, inspecting it. "They stopped using these in 2003. Now they use a MetroCard." Dad held his up for Christie to see.

Christie marveled at the sheer numbers of people getting on and off. Their stop came, and they joined the jam of people. Dad and Junior seemed to wend their way through them effortlessly, but Christie had to jump out of the way often.

How do they do this day after day? No wonder Dad takes a limo.

At Dad's office, he gave them a tour of the trading desk. A few people sat at desks, doing something. Each station had four big screens in front of the trader and a huge phone button bank. She had no idea how it all worked or what it would be like during trading hours.

Dad said, "I need to catch up on a few things. You two go on, and I'll meet you back home for dinner."

They exited to the city and its delights. The Statue of Liberty made it to the list, as did the Intrepid Air Museum. They spent the day touring, seeing the sights, walking for miles, returning tired.

They spent the night like the night before, him kissing her, then holding her until they slept, dreamless this night.

*****

Christie

Sunday was their travel day, and they were to be wheels-up at noon. Three hours later, they were home in Petoskey. He drove her home, kissing her for a long time as he dropped her off and said, "How about dinner together tomorrow. I like being with you all the time."

In the foreground, she said, "I like that too," but her mind flowed with, *We can't keep doing this. It's a façade, you and me. I'm from the other side of the tracks. We can't be together. It'll never work. I'm trash compared to you.*

Christie worked to keep up a happy front. Norman was oblivious to her thoughts, happy, bouncing on his toes.

"Good. Come to my house at five or so, after work, and I'll fix us dinner."

She tried to look eager, keeping her shoulders from sagging. "I'll be there," is what she said, but thought, *And we'll be through when I tell you.*

Chapter 11

Christie

C hristie drove to his house with her stomach churning, practicing a speech to give to him, that they would never work, and they were through. Backing her car into the parking place to give her a quick getaway, she left it running. Ringing the bell, he opened the door, smiling. She could not look at him as she entered partway, keeping the door open.

With a happy voice, Norman said, "Dad had so much fun with you, he already thinks of you as a daughter and asked us to New York for Christmas. It's magical then." He moved to kiss her, but she stopped him with a hand on his chest.

"You need to listen to me. Promise me that you'll say nothing until I finish, okay?" she said, staring into his eyes, trying not to cry.

"Okay?" he replied, surprise filling his voice.

The door was still open when she began her speech.

"I saw what it was all like in New York, that we could never work. I'm an embarrassment to you, a girl from the wrong side of the tracks, and I'll never fit in there. I can't be with you because I'll ruin you. You need to be with those high society women, like Cybill. You'll like them, with big boobs, who can sparkle in the parties and talk their talk. We can't be together, so I'm leaving you before I ruin you or embarrass you or your Dad. He's so nice, and I don't want to hurt him. I love you both, but I'm trash in your circles. I'm just trash."

Turning on her heel, she fled out the door, jumped in her car, and sped away.

*****

Norman

Norman was left in the doorway, watching her car disappear down the road with his mouth open, blinking, in shock.

He went back over her words, thinking about them.

The wrong side of the tracks, high society women, big boobs, sparkle at parties, talk the talk, embarrass him or Dad, she is trash.

He paused, his mind still reeling from her words.

What? She's talking nonsense. What's she thinking?

He felt his back pocket, but no phone. Slamming the door shut, he raced upstairs, found his phone and called her. The call went right to voicemail. Waiting for fifteen minutes, he tried again with the same result. An hour later gave the same result.

He thought about her words.

The women in the box must have said something to her, or she overheard something. No. I know some of those women, and they wouldn't think that. Rather, they could be her friends. They would love to know her. What's she thinking?

Pacing the floor, he tried another call—the same result.

We have different backgrounds, maybe that's it. New York was such a shock that she snapped under the weight of the difference?

He vowed to call her every hour until midnight to get an answer.

*****

Christie

Tears dripped from her cheeks the whole way to her house. She burst into it, seeing the shabbiness of it, flew to her room and bed, going into a fetal position, hugging her pillow and sobbing. Feeling her phone buzz in her back pocket, she pulled it out, turning it off, crying herself to sleep.

She woke hungry at about eight p.m. and fixed herself a frozen dinner, eating it solely to keep her stomach from bothering her, weeping as she ate. Her relationship with Norman had sunk into the sea like Atlantis, never to be seen again.

I need to move, to get away from him in this tiny town. Perhaps I could move to Chicago, to Karen, my friend, who's still single. Possibly I could live with her for a while until I find my footing there.

Getting into her pajamas, she remembered their love-times together, how special they were, how loved she felt. The difference from then to now brought on a fresh round of sobbing.

*****

Norman

Norman tried calling her more times, starting at six a.m. to see if she would answer. Nothing. He called Mable at "Hire a Temp" to see if she called in for an assignment. She said, "Yes, she called in about seven, but I don't have anything for her today."

"Okay, thanks."

At least she was answering someone's calls. His day was light, mostly catching up from being gone over Thanksgiving, so Christie became his focus. He couldn't remember the name of her friend who he met in the restaurant. He tried calling more, but still, no answer.

At noon, he called Mable back and said, "Could you please call Christie. We've been seeing each other for some time now."

"I know. I heard that, and I was glad for both of you."

"Thanks, but for some reason, she broke up with me."

With an edge, Mable asked, "Did you treat her poorly?"

"No. We just returned from New York, where we saw my dad. We had a great time, I thought."

"Hmmm. Do you know why she chose to break up with you?"

"She rambled on about not working together, from being from different sides of the tracks."

"Well, that's for sure true, but it shouldn't stop you two from being together. She could adapt to your wealth." Mable knew everything about everyone. She was the best source for secret information if you could worm it from her. Chocolate worked well if it was high quality, like Godiva.

"Could you call her. She doesn't answer when I call. See what happened; how can I make it right?"

"Old Matchmaker Mable will give it a try. But I'm going to have to charge you for my services as a temp of the love type."

"Thanks so much. I'll pay whatever. I want her back. I need her back. Let me know what she says."

*****

Christie

"Christie, how are you?"

"Awful. Mable, I'm leaving, moving away, so I can't afflict Norman."

"What? How are you an affliction to him?"

"Our economic situations are too different. I can't fit into his side; I'll only embarrass him and his dad. I have to leave."

"Christie, that's nonsense. You two are good together. You can adapt to anything; I know that about you. You can adapt to his wealthy ways."

"No. I'll embarrass him. I'm trash in his eyes."

"Did he tell you that."

"Ummm, no. Not him, but his friends think of me that way. I'll never fit in with them."

"Did you hear them say that about you?"

"Well, no, but I had a dream that they did, two dreams actually. In the second one, they were cutting me up with machetes."

"What? You believe a dream when, in reality, you never heard anyone say anything like that?"

"Yes. My dreams tell me lots of things. I listen to them."

"Well, you need to forget those two. They're lying to you."

"No. I think they're the reality of our situation. My relationship with him is like Atlantis. It sank into the sea, never to be seen or found again."

"Christie, Christie, your thinking is all wrong, can't you see that?"

"No. I'm leaving. Actually, I'm already on the road, headed for a friend. Norman and I are over, and I need to get away from him." She lied, but in an hour, it would be the truth. Packing and talking were simultaneous.

"There is nothing I can say to change your mind?"

"No. I have to be away from him, so I don't embarrass him somehow."

"Well, I'm sorry to see you go, and I think you're making a huge mistake."

"No, no mistake. I can't be with him anymore."

"Okay, bye."

"Mable, thanks for everything."

*****

Norman

"Norman, she left, moved out, and is on her way to a friend's somewhere," Mable said.

"What? That can't be. She can't be gone."

"Well, she is. She doesn't want to embarrass you or your dad with her other side of the tracks ways. So, to protect you, she left."

"That's just crazy. I love her. I need her. Where can I find her?"

"Norman, I don't know, but I hear you. Good luck."

He wrestled with what to do, pacing his living room floor. Going to her house, her car was gone. Pounding on her door brought no results. He drove back home despondent, shoulders sagged, face fallen, listless, without a solution to the problem.

Chapter 12

Christie

C hristie had never known such pain. She intended to drive straight through to Karen's apartment near Midway Airport. It should take about six hours — six hours of agony, weeping, anger, pounding the wheel with her fist, regretting her decision, then reinstating it again. She called Karen as she drove, but she would not be home from work until five-thirty. Christie slowed her pace, stopping for snacks and lunch, staying away from people who would wonder about her moods, and arrived about six.

Karen hugged her and wanted to hear the whole story. Christie blurted it all out. Karen listened, asked some questions for clarification, and when it was all out, she said, "I think you made a mistake in leaving. Your dreams are from your imagination, not reality. Did those women say things like that?"

"Well, no. They were friendly, but I was so beneath them."

"How so?"

"Well, they had Kate Spade purses and rocks on their fingers the size of an egg. Their business casual was way above my finest dress outfit. They had big boobs, probably fake, but they showed them off. They thought differently, with money, and they talked differently."

"Did you listen to them? Did you talk to them?"

"Yeah."

"Did they sound normal, like you?"

111

"Yeah, but I know that they're way different. They probably just talked down to me."

"Christie, that's an assumption. All of what you have told me is an assumption. You're making a mistake."

Her phone buzzed.

"Who is that?"

She looked at it, and it was him. "Norman."

"Then, answer it."

"No." She swiped to disconnect the call.

"Next time he calls, I'm going to answer it and talk to him for you."

"No, you're not. I'll throw my phone into the toilet."

"You're just as stubborn as I remembered."

Christie glared daggers at her.

"Let's go out and get some margaritas and Mexican. You can drown your sorrows in alcohol."

Christie softened with that suggestion.

"Good idea."

Leaving her phone behind, Christie and Karen escaped to south of the border, to tequila and chips with salsa.

*****

Norman

Norman was beside himself, pacing the floor when he was awake, thrashing in his bed when he tried to sleep. He had no contact with her at all, though her phone did ring. Saturday dawned to desperation. About nine the next morning, he decided to call his father.

"Junior, great to hear from you. What brought this call on?"

Norman paced the floor. "Dad, Christie left me and left town as well. She disappeared, going to a friend's somewhere out of Petoskey. She won't answer my calls."

He sat on his sofa, staring at a framed selfie of them on Isle Royale.

"What? I thought you two were doing well together. It seemed that way when you were here."

"I thought so, but Monday night, after we returned, I invited her for dinner, and she gave me a speech of how we're so different, economically, socially, and can't be together. She was trash in her eyes, compared to me, and doesn't want to embarrass either of us."

"Um-hmm."

"She spoke her piece, turned on her heel, and fled from me." Norman stood, pacing again.

"You don't know this, but when your mother and I met, we were in a similar situation. She was from a poor family, and as you know, our family was wealthy. We met at a dance, and I fell in love with her from the first minute I saw her. I convinced her to go out with me, but after a while, our different situations got in the way, and she did what Christie did, she broke up with me. Fortunately, then, it was harder for people to leave, they were less mobile, so I found her and persuaded her to get back together. It worked, and we married, to the frustration of my parents, but over time, they grew to love her like a daughter, loving her almost more than me. Let me call her and see if I can reason with her."

Norman sat again, relieved that his father would help him.

"Dad, thanks so much for helping me. I never knew that about Mom."

"She didn't advertise it, but once we married, she helped her parents into a house, and we put her siblings through college. They turned out wonderfully, all of them professional people of one sort or another. I keep in touch with all of them, and once every five years, we get together, even with their sister now gone. The shocker was Maggie's mother, Agnes. Once she became connected with our family, her wisdom and intelligence for business emerged, and she became a tycoon in her own right, using family money to amass her own fortune."

He paused. "Let me call Christie and get back to you."

"Thanks, Dad."

*****

Christie

Christie texted Samantha. They had not talked since their exchange when she and Norman first met and missed her companionship. She didn't expect a response for a while, because she would be at work.

Christie's phone rang. Karen grabbed it and answered.

"Hi, Christie. This is Norman Peale senior."

"Sir, this is her friend, Karen."

114

"Oh, is she there?"

Christie heard the word "Norman" and began to shake her head violently and back away toward the bathroom and a door that would lock. Muffling the phone, Karen said, "It's Senior."

Christie stopped. "Really? Senior? What could he want? Norman said that he asked us to New York for Christmas. Maybe he wants to ask me personally?"

Christie took her phone and said, "Mr. Peale, hi."

"Christie, please, call me Dad. I insist."

"Okay." Christie moved to sit on the sofa.

"Junior called me and said you broke up with him."

"Ummm. Yes."

"Junior also told me some of the words you used in your speech to him."

"Ummm. Okay."

"I need to tell you that the woman I married came from the other side of the tracks compared to my family as you think of yourself compared to Junior."

"Really?" Christie stood.

"Yes. And, she broke up with me, like you just did with Junior."

"She did?" Christie walked over to the window and peered out, seeing nothing.

"Yes, but she could not run as you did, she didn't have a car, so I found her and wooed her back, and after a year, we were married."

"Really?"

"Yes, though my parents didn't like it, I told them that it was my decision whom I married, so they needed to get used to it."

"You said that to them?"

"Yes, and they accepted it, after talking to my grandfather, who stuck up for me."

"He did?" Christie moved back to the sofa and sat.

"And, we were happily married for all those years. My parents, who initially rejected her, grew to love her, more than they loved me, I think. She became a daughter to them."

"Oh my. That's wonderful." Christie's shoulders sagged in relief, and she exhaled a big breath.

"Yes, and I think you're making a huge mistake by running from Junior."

"I'm not so sure. I'm trash compared to him." Her face turned sad at the thought, and her shoulders sagged in resignation.

"Christie Yaeger, that's utter nonsense and a total lie. I saw who you are, and you're his equal in every way but money, which can be lost in an instant. If the money is gone, what do you have? You're matched and good together. Money or no money, you belong with him, and he belongs with you. I saw you together in my home. I know love when I see it."

Christie's shoulders sunk in resignation and hope. "Oh, Dad, do you really think so?" Emotion filled her voice, tears filling her eyes as she spoke.

"I know so."

"I want that, but I'm afraid of being an embarrassment to him, or you."

116

"Maggie was never an embarrassment to me, rather the reverse. I needed her to keep me in line."

Christie's countenance changed; she laughed and said, "I can't imagine that. She must have been an amazing woman."

"For sure, she was, and so are you, I'm sure of it."

Can it be true that Norman and I can be together despite our differences? Can we be like his dad and mom? Gads, I made a huge mistake, causing all this mess.

He paused. "I've sent a jet to Petoskey to get Junior and bring him to you. Text him where you are. You'll see him tonight sometime. I'll text you an approximate time from the pilot once he's on board. Have a reunion. I remember what mine was like when I persuaded my Maggie to come back to me. Then, drive back to Petoskey and come to see me at Christmas. New York is magical that time of year."

Christie's heart fluttered with the news. Atlantis had perhaps not sunk, forever, and seem to be rising, even now, water draining from its streets.

"Okay, Dad. Thanks so much for telling me all this. I want this to work between Norman and me. I'll wait to hear from you, and I'll text him my address."

"Good. See you soon."

Karen regarded her friend, who was now all smiles and happy. "You seem different."

"Yeah, I am. A jet is going to Petoskey to get Norman and bring him here to me, to have a reunion."

Karen had listened and said, "Oh, I love money and what it can make happen."

Christie bounced on her toes. "Dad said he would text me when Norman will land once the pilot knows."

"I like how you call him Dad. Perhaps he is a replacement for your real Dad."

"Yes, he is."

Her phone dinged, and she looked at it, a text from Dad. It gave only a time, eight-thirty, about two hours from then.

Christie's hands shook in excitement. "I need to change. I didn't bring much."

"Let's go see what you brought and pick something."

Christie took a shower and dressed in the finest of what she had. Karen did her nails, shaped them, and put on a red polish. Christie had to hold her hand still with her other hand because she shook in anticipation. With five minutes to go, she stood by the window, which could see the street, pacing, wringing her hands. Just a little late, a limo pulled up to the curb.

Chapter 13

Christie

Christie waited until the door opened and could see that it was him. She shrieked, "He's here," and bolted for the door, leaving it open and flew down the stairs. Karen shook her head, smiling, calling after her, "I'll be down in a minute after locking my door."

*****

Norman

As she emerged from the entrance, Norman thought, *There's my girl. I'm so glad to find her.*

Three feet from him, she launched herself at him, webbing him in arms and legs, knocking him back against the car from her momentum. Her lips landed on his almost with the force of a punch, kissing him frantically. Each time she parted, she said, "I love you."

When her frenzy slowed, she parted, and he said, "It's nice to see you, and I love you too."

Really nice to find her. I was lost without her, in agony.

Karen watched them and said, "I guess you two haven't seen each other for a while."

Norman looked at her and said, "Understatement."

Christie continued to kiss him. Still supporting her, he let her feet slip to the ground, saying to Karen, "Thanks, so, so much, for caring for my girl. We'll be downtown for a few days; then we'll come back for her car and things."

"I was glad to help."

Opening the limo door for Christie, he said, once inside, "I've chosen a restaurant for our reunion celebration, then we have a room at the Intercontinental Downtown Magnificent Mile for a few days."

Christie nodded, her face covered with a grin and sparkling eyes. They partied with marvelous food and champagne until the restaurant closed.

Outside walking, holding her hand, he turned to Christie, got close to her smiling face and said, "Christie Yaeger, we're going to a hotel for several days, and I'm going to make love to you each day, maybe more than once, to convince you that you're the woman for me, my woman. I want to convince you that your boobs are precisely the size and sensitivity for me, what I want, that the rest of your body is perfect for me, that I love your body, and I love you, all of you, everything about you, your mind, your heart, your soul, your body, everything."

"Norman, that sounds wonderful," her grin was from ear to ear.

He stroked her cheek with the back of his fingers, then touched her lips. "Christie, I love you. You need to know and trust that."

Smiling, a finger on his chest, she replied, "I love you too. Thanks for coming to rescue me from a huge mistake."

His eyes turned liquid. "I thought I lost you, so I called Dad. He told me about his experience with Mom. I never knew that about them." Tears leaked from his eyes. Christie touched them with her finger.

"He told me the same thing, and it got to me, convincing me that we could work."

He sniffed a couple of times, "First things first, to the Intercontinental and bed."

"Oh, Norman, I have none of my things. They're all at Karen's."

He grinned.

That's perfect.

"Tonight, my darling, you won't need any, just your birthday suit."

*****

Christie

Christie giggled and had to turn away from his eyes, but quickly came back to them.

It's happening. It's happening. He's going to make love to me, to break our boundaries and claim me as his woman above all the others. This is perfect.

Smiling, gazing into her eyes, he said, "Tomorrow, we'll go shopping, and you'll be equipped with everything, the equal of those New York women, though we'll collect your things and your car from Karen's place."

Taking her by the hand, he led her a short way to their hotel. The reservation was for one of the penthouse suites. They had no luggage, only Norman's backpack. When they entered it, she gasped from the view and the grandeur, even a gas fireplace. She turned to him with wide eyes and asked, "Can we make love by the fireplace. I wanted to when we were in our cabin on Isle Royale, but it was too fast."

"Absolutely. I'd love that idea. We'll make a bed right there." He pointed. "Then, I want to undress you and make love to you for a long time, to take you to the moon and back."

Her eyes went distant, out over the city, but came back to Norman. They went to the bedroom, laughing, helping each other, bringing blankets, and the quilt to the fireplace, making a bed of sorts. The city lights, the rising moon, and the dancing firelight illuminated them. He turned her around so that he could undress her from behind, to caress her as he undid buttons, unzipped zippers, slipping her clothes from her. Lifting her, he set her onto their bed, covering her with the quilt.

The fire hissed and popped as he disrobed and lay next to her, having hid himself to give some mystery. She knew what would happen next but had only a little idea of how.

"Birth control?"

"My period is about to start in a couple of days, so we're pretty safe."

Norman nodded. "Are you willing to risk it?"

"Yeah. I want you naturally."

Here we go; this is it. I love him so.

Part-Time Worker, Full-Time Lover

He began with kisses, but she sensed these were different somehow, kisses of commitment and passion. His hand started in her hair, brushing her ear, but moved down to her breast, circling it, moving uphill until his fingers surrounded her nipple, turning it, lifting it, arousing her.

He gave her a silent kiss on her ear and whispered, "I'm taking you from the earth," he gave her nipple a tender caress, "to the moon and back, this way." Twiddling her nipple, he left, drawing with his finger in a slow clockwise spiral down her right breast, across her cleavage, and in a counter-clockwise spiral up her left breast to her nipple which he surrounded with his fingers. "Just like a NASA moon shot."

That made her laugh.

Twiddling her nipple, he whispered, "You laugh. Just wait, and you'll see."

Gazing into his eyes, she hushed, "Can't wait. It feels so good."

His mouth went to her left side and his fingers to her right. The explosion of pleasure in her made her gasp, her back arched and her head sank back into the pillow.

He rose and whispered, "Sensitive as always."

Between pantings, she could only mumble, "Mmmm-hmmm."

He raised and moved between her legs. Latching onto her right side, he took into his mouth as much of her breast as he could, letting it slide out, wet and slippery. Her moans and body movements displayed her pleasure, which encouraged him to give to her more.

His kisses and caresses meandered down her body, all the way to her secret garden. Inside her garden, he found her special spot that ignited her arousal, and she roared upward, up and up, until she exploded like a skyrocket, grunting as he caressed her, back arched, head back, mouth open, gripping the bedding in her fists, clamping him with her legs.

After letting her descend, further caresses there flew her to a higher climax, and then a third brought a shriek of pleasure from her mouth as she melted into release.

Joined to her, they moved in tandem until he erupted in his own release. Laying at her side, covered by the quilt, they rested, floating down like feathers with him caressing her breast.

When their eyes opened, though hers seemed like they couldn't focus, he whispered, "So, how was that for you."

"Oh, Norman, it was unbelievable. I've never experienced anything so wonderful, ever."

"Good, because we're not done, though I want to finish in bed where we can sleep comfortably."

"I can't move."

"Not a problem, I'll carry you."

He moved to their bed, pulled the covers down, returned to her, lifted her, and carried her to bed. Joining her, he latched onto her left side, and his fingers found her secret garden. He caressed her to two more climaxes, and in the last, she almost screamed from pleasure.

He released her, resting at her side, caressing her breast, letting her descend. After a time, he rolled to his back, and she rolled to snuggle with him. Her eyes never opened before sleep took her.

He whispered, "That's my girl, pleasured into oblivion."

Chapter 14

Christie

Rising about eleven, they showered together, washing each other. Christie clung to him as they walked the few blocks to Saks Fifth Avenue.

His hand on her back, Norman smiled and asked one of the clerks, "Could we possibly speak to the manager?"

Presently, he stood before them, introducing himself. "Is there a problem?"

Norman smiled at him, shaking his hand, saying, "Not at all, rather the reverse. I'm Norman Peale. Do you see this beautiful woman?"

Christie straightened her posture, smiling, trying to look beautiful.

The man regarded her, nodding. "Yes, she is indeed beautiful."

Christie blushed, and Norman rubbed her back with his hand.

"Well, we need to outfit her with everything, from head to toe. She has nothing, other than what she's wearing. We need a complete wardrobe, elegant to casual, and all the accessories."

The man's eyes showed shock as if such words were rarely spoken in his store, but then dilated, anticipating a huge bill. Then, he smiled broadly, rubbing his hands together.

I think he's salivating at Norman's suggestion.

"And we're the store that can help you accomplish that."

Norman's smiled widened, and he pulled Christie to his hip. "I thought so. Could you possibly give us a person to guide us through your departments?"

If this were a grade B movie, the manager would make a fantastic dastardly villain.

Still smiling broadly, he said, "Certainly. Harriette is our most experienced salesperson, having been with us for many years. She can help you in every department." Turning to his clerk, he whispered to her, with her hurrying to a phone.

Within a few minutes, Harriette appeared, an attractive, fifty-something woman, impeccably dressed.

Gesturing to Christie, the manager said to her, "This woman needs a complete wardrobe, head to toe, everything."

To Norman and Christie, he said, "Harriette will take good care of you."

Harriette turned to Christie, sizing her up. "Let's start at the beginning, Lingerie. Come with me." They chatted as they walked about her tastes in colors, styles, and patterns, dress size, shoe size, makeup, everything. Norman followed behind, the paying agent and cart pusher.

In Lingerie, Norman found a chair while the women shopped. As they looked at nightwear, Christie called to Norman, "No peeking at what I select."

"No way. I like the mystery."

Both Christie and Harriette laughed and continued their search.

Christie noticed Norman approaching one of the clerks, and presently a cart appeared, into which went several boxes.

In charge of pushing the cart, Norman called out, "On to the next department," which made Christie laugh.

Time passed, and Harriette proved to be an able fashion consultant. Christie and Harriette planned a wardrobe of elegant clothes, casual clothes, and business casual, all with matching jewelry, new makeup, and perfumes, shoes to match her outfits, everything. Christie looked to Norman for approval and had him take pictures of her in every outfit, so she could remember them. When a cart filled, it was taken to the shipping department to be sent to Petoskey, except for a few casual clothes for use while in Chicago, and a few nightwear items too.

One of the dresses she chose was bright red, off her shoulders, gorgeous. Remembering their first meeting, Norman asked Harriett to bring a bright red lipstick, which she applied and posed with Norman, borrowing some roses from a nearby vase. Christie looked stunning. Harriett's hand was at her mouth, in awe of her beauty. Norman kissed her cheek and said, "This is the dress for a public appearance. You are so beautiful."

Christie regarded herself in a mirror and agreed. Never had she worn something so marvelous, elegant, and sophisticated.

I'll wow them in the Big Apple.

They took Harriette to a late lunch in their restaurant, and they chatted about their lives, sharing how they got to this point in their relationship. Harriette's husband passed some years ago. She mourned for a year but came back to work, and it rescued her from grief. She was glad to help people like them.

After lunch, they continued, and by late afternoon, they finished, accumulated a sizable bill, had most of their purchases shipped to Petoskey, but kept some as casual clothes for here. Christie was exhausted.

I never thought shopping could be such hard work. Whew.

Walking to their hotel, arm in arm, she clung to him. "Thank you for all my clothes."

"You look marvelous in them and will be the talk of New York when we go for Christmas."

"Do you really think so? I don't want to embarrass you or Dad. He told me that his wife kept him in line."

"She did, as I remember. He couldn't leave the house without her approval of his suit and tie. She would make him change if she didn't approve."

Christie laughed as they walked toward their hotel.

*****

Norman

Norman pondered the day as Christie disappeared into the bathroom to change for bed. He lit the fire and made a bed like the night before, changing into his sleep shorts as he waited.

What's happened in the last two days? Christie and I are reconnected and closer than ever. My heart is convinced she's the woman for me, the love of my life. We made love last night, right here by the fire and it was wonderful, my best ever because I'm so in love with her. I want to give her anything and everything. We shopped till she dropped, but now she is prepared for

128

anything, looking elegant and beautiful in any setting. I love everything about her—mind, soul, and body. She's the woman I want at my side always.

Emerging in a pink unlined corded lace teddy, she struck a model's pose in the bathroom door, one hand raised, the other on her hip. Norman's mouth fell open.

"Harriette helped me pick this out for us."

A hand under his chin, he closed his mouth, making Christie giggle. "And, a fabulous choice it is."

Christie ambled toward him in a runway walk, swaying her body, moving her hands seductively along her sides, staring into his eyes. Her outfit was mostly see-through with thin straps in the back, lots of skin visible. As she walked, she pirouetted, letting him see all of her. He wolf-whistled. She would turn, walk away for a step, turn, and then walk toward him. By the time she got to him, he was salivating.

I've never seen so beautiful a woman.

"Christie, you're gorgeous."

A sly smile on her face, blowing him a Marilyn Monroe kiss, she breathed, "Thought you might like it."

He helped her lay on her back, lying next to her, his hands floating over her body, brushing her, enticing her out of ordinary life. His lips joined hers as he caressed her, letting her float upward. The light from the fire danced on her body, enhancing his view of her. Slipping her shoulder straps down, he began to reveal her delights, slowly with many caresses and kisses, whispering words of love, arousing her more.

One pleasure spot led to another with Christie moaning, panting, arching her back, head back into the pillow, mouth open wide until release claimed her, flowing through her in waves. Two more climaxes and he let her float down to open her eyes.

She whispered, "I want to send you to the moon tonight. On your back, my love."

She pleasured him in every way with him moaning, arching his back at the moment of his release deep inside her, his hands on her breasts.

"Norman, I love you."

Still in his reverie, he panted out, "I—love—you—too."

She let him recover, then whispered, "Let's move to our bed."

"Yeah."

At her side, more caresses sent her high into the mountains of climax-ecstasy until his hands stilled on her body, letting her float back to earth.

When I pleasure her to a climax, it gives me almost as much pleasure as my own release. That's how much I love this woman.

*****

Christie

They spent the next three days seeing the town, museums, the Planetarium, walking Michigan Avenue and State Street, going up in the Willis Tower at night, looking out at the lights. Norman hired a small plane from Chicago Executive to take them around the city. He convinced their pilot, for a sizable tip, to give Christie a flying lesson. Flying out over the water, he taught her how to recover from a stall. She screamed the first time they spun, out of control, nose down for the lake. But he recovered easily, and after five tries, she did the same. Norman could see her glow like a firefly when they landed; her eyes showed him. The pilot took a picture of them together with the plane.

Each night, he made love to her, by the fire and in bed, sailing her way past the moon and back, sometimes again if they woke during the night.

I'm so happy, smoothed out by his love for me and his making love to me. Could anything be better than this? I look at him, and he's the same as me, so in love with me. He's happy and wanting to love on me all the time. This is perfect.

Somewhere in their stay, she heard back from Samantha, who was apologetic for having said what she did. Obviously, Norman was different with Christie than he had been in the gossip rags. She wished them well.

A limo took them back to Karen's apartment to get her things and her car. Karen took one look at clingy, smoothed out, elegantly dressed Christie and said, "I'm glad you two are back together. Money works wonders to make a woman look good." Gathering her things, they packed her car. Karen hugged them goodbye, and off they went.

As he drove them back to Petoskey, they talked about birth control.

"Now that you're making love to me, which makes me really happy, by the way, I want us to be as natural as we can. My married friends use an IUD once they were done having kids, and they love it. I want to get one for me."

"Okay."

"I'll make an appointment when we get back."

They arrived at his office to a small mountain of boxes from Saks Fifth Avenue. The phoenix of their relationship had risen.

Chapter 15

Christie

Christie asked Norman, "Who will cook Christmas dinner for us?"

"Arthur, Dad's chef. You met him. Usually, we have it on Christmas Eve so Arthur can be with his family on Christmas Day."

"I have an idea. Let's give Arthur the time off to be with his family and cook the dinner ourselves. I can cook, and if you two help me, we'll get it done and have fun together in the process."

"That's a grand idea. Let's call Dad."

Norman dialed, put his phone on speaker, and said, "Dad, Christie has an idea that I like. Give Arthur the day off to be with his family, and we cook Christmas dinner, ourselves, on Christmas Day. It'll be fun."

"That's a wonderful idea. Have Christie text me her menu, and I'll ask Arthur to order the ingredients, as he knows the best places for meat and produce."

Christie spoke, "Let's have Prime Rib and let Arthur choose the sides to go with it. If it's something unusual, he can give me a recipe. And, I want to have cherry pie for dessert."

"That sounds wonderful. I'll tell him, and it will be ready when you arrive. He'll appreciate the time with his family."

Norman said, "See you, Dad, on the twenty-second."

"Great. I'm looking forward to it."

The call disconnected, Christie said, "I have another question. What do you do for Christmas presents? You both have everything you want or can buy. What do you do?"

Norman laughed and said, "Usually, not much, maybe a CD or DVD. Dad puts up a tree, for tradition, but there is little under it. Mom, when she was alive, organized a few gifts, but neither of us needed more stuff."

"Okay, got the idea." Christie had a plan for them both.

*****

Christie

The plane, with Tom, Theodore, and Joan as their flight crew, flew them to Teterboro Airport on December 22. Christie dressed in a new business casual outfit but looked elegant. Norman was so proud of her and so proud to be with her as they traveled. Joan noticed the difference in her clothes, saying, "You look different from when we last met."

"Yeah. We've had some adventures since Thanksgiving. I'll tell you about it once we're airborne."

Spending some time with Joan, Christie related their adventures. She could see Joan as a friend.

The limo took them to Dad's building, and he met them when they rang his bell. He ushered them in, and upon seeing Christie out of her coat, said, "Junior said that you got some new clothes. Christie, you look wonderful, elegant, and part of high society, just gorgeous."

Blushing at his admiration, she whispered, "Thanks. It was all Norman. He insisted on dressing me at Saks in Chicago."

"And an excellent job he did. My wife, Maggie, shopped there many times here in New York. She always looked wonderful, elegant when she returned."

Christie surrounded Norman with her arm, pulling him to herself.

Dad continued, "I'm so pleased that you two are still together. Come in and rest yourselves with some wine, Gewürztraminer, like we had at Thanksgiving."

Christie's eyes opened wide, and she said, "I'd love that."

"We need to celebrate your new look and all of us together here at Christmas. I know a place that would be perfect. Let me call for a reservation."

Dad made a call, and they had a table at seven-thirty p.m. Sitting with their wine, they talked about their separation and rescue flight. Dad listened intently, but his eyes would go distant as their story meshed with his own.

Dad had put up a Christmas tree, artificial, twelve feet tall, splendidly decorated. Someone did it, but no matter, it looked gorgeous. She had a thought and went to Norman, her lips to his ear, "Make love to me by the Christmas tree, on Christmas Eve."

Turning to her, kissing her, he whispered, "I'd love to do that."

"It would be such a grand memory from here."

Little did she know of the plans he had for her on the 'morrow.

135

They had a fabulous dinner, and Christie noticed that men and women surveyed her, even some women subtly pointing in her direction. Some say that clothes make the man. Well, they make the woman as well. Her confidence was on the ceiling because she was beautiful, equal with those women around her. They stayed late, sipping wine and sampling desserts, fit for a king. Laughing, they even sang with the strolling violinist when he came by their table. They had a grand celebration.

The limo took them home, and Junior walked with Christie, his hand on her back, a comfortable position for them. As the door to their room closed, he said, "I'm not going to make love to you tonight, as I have a surprise for you tomorrow. The appointment is at ten."

"A surprise? Tell me!"

"No way. It's a complete surprise, but I think you'll like it."

Kissing him and rubbing her body on him to try to unlock his lips revealed nothing.

He whispered, "Turn around, so I can undress you sensually."

"Not too much, or I'll make love to you."

Laughing, he said, "Only a little playing with your body."

He undressed her with caresses, which made her coo at him, helped her into her sleepwear with more caresses, and then into bed.

She slid toward him and whispered, "Thank you for all you've done for me. It makes me feel confident and beautiful. I'm not afraid of the other women now."

"I'm so glad."

"I love you, Norman."

"Christie, I love you too."

She rolled to lay on him.

A naïve Christie thought, *What can his surprise be? I don't know.*

Chapter 16

Christie

They stood at the limo as the doorman opened the door. Norman held out a strip of cloth, which he told her was a blindfold. Her eyes covered; he helped her into the car, and away they went. After some time, the limo stopped, and Norman said, "We're here. Let me help you out."

"Okay."

His hand on her back, caressing her, he led her into a store through two doors, her shoes clacking on the stone tile. She tried to listen to anything that would give it away, but it was silent as a tomb. Leaving her for just a moment, he returned, took her hand into his, and from below her ears, she heard him say, "Okay, lift the blindfold."

There he was on one knee, holding her hand saying, "Christie Yaeger, I have loved you since we first met. Will you do me the immense honor of becoming my wife?"

Christie looked at him, her mouth open, then looked around. They were in a jewelry store, and the words on the wall read, "Harry Winston." She knew who that was and what they purveyed. The attendant men and women watched them, some of the women with hands to their mouths, one took pictures, another video. Processing his words, she realized what he asked. Tears filled her eyes, and she choked out, "Yes. I'll marry you. I love you so much."

He stood, she grabbed him, and peppered him with kisses, saying, "I love you," each time she parted.

When she released him, he said, "We're here to get you an engagement ring. This store should have something you'll like."

"Do ducks quack?"

Laughing at her comment, he said, "I asked Karen and Samantha what stone you liked the best, and they both said sapphires, especially a light color. Light blue sapphires are rare, but this establishment has excellent contacts, and they have something for you to consider."

The attendants sprang into action, bringing a velvet tray with a wedding ring set of a large central diamond surrounded by pale blue sapphires. Also, on the tray was a necklace more gorgeous than Christie had ever seen, a mix of diamonds and pale blue sapphires. Next to the necklace rested a pair of earrings in a similar design, dangles covered in diamonds and sapphires, but not too long.

Norman gestured to the tray and said, "Try them on."

An attendant, with Sally on her name tag, helped her, then took her to a mirror. As they finished, she whispered into Christie's ear, "They look gorgeous on you."

Christie agreed wholeheartedly, but she had seen the price tag, $127,500. She turned to Norman with a look of horror on her face and said, "I don't make that much in five years, even if I had no expenses."

Smiling broadly, touching her arm, he countered, "I know, but I make that much in about two weeks with expenses. And, I'm paying the bill. I think they're stunning on you."

"But, I can't wear these around for every day. Could I get an artificial pair of earrings and a ring for everyday use?"

Sally responded, "Almost everyone says the same thing. A color-matched zirconia set of earrings and the wedding ring set is included with the ensemble."

Norman regarded Christie with the set, had her turn various ways to see her in the light, and asked, "Do you like them?"

"Do turkeys gobble?"

He laughed, as did Sally, and he said, "I'll take that as a yes."

He said to Sally, "We'll buy. Please put them on my account, and we'll take them with us."

"Of course, Mr. Peale."

Christie looked at him in astonishment, saying, "You have an account here?"

"Sure. Everyone needs an account at Harry Winston. You never know when an occasion will come up where a significant piece of jewelry is needed."

Christie laughed and said, "If you say so."

"But, we need to make my question and your answer official." Plucking the engagement ring from the tray, he lowered to one knee, and said, "Christie Yaeger, I love you so much; will you be my wife?"

She stared deep into his eyes and said, "Yes, I'd love to be your wife, and I love you too."

He slipped the ring onto her finger, a perfect fit. She touched it, feeling of the stones and the connection between them that the ring represented. Sally put their purchases into plush boxes and brought them in a small bag with Harry Winston embossed in gold letters, and they exited, thanking Sally and the others for their help. Mission accomplished.

Chapter 17

Christie

The limo took them back home, and Christie modeled her purchase for Dad. He said, "They add to your beauty and look gorgeous on you. I've always liked Harry Winston, and I'm glad you can wear something of theirs."

After a pause, he continued, "Today is the 23rd, so let's see something of the magic of New York at Christmas, and let's do it together. I have a list of the most interesting places to visit. Let's hit the streets."

The limo waited for them, and they spent the day seeing the sights of New York decorated for Christmas and eating in marvelous places, like a progressive dinner, one restaurant after another, course by course.

As they walked, he whispered into her ear, "You know, I'm with the most beautiful woman in the city, my woman, my life partner, with a ring on her finger, my claim on her. You, your person, fills my heart with joy and makes me feel complete as a man."

Christie's heart leaped for joy. No man had said such words to her, ever. She turned to him and kissed him as they walked, responding, "I'm so glad. Since we met, I've always wanted to be so for you."

Christie took pictures and selfies of the three of them as a memory. She wanted to make picture-books for Junior and Dad, to remember their time. This was her most magical Christmas ever. Sally had taken a series of pictures of their proposal and sent them to Christie's phone. Vickie took a video on Norman's phone to be added to the magic of today.

Late Christmas Eve, after Dad went to bed, they gathered blankets and a sheet to make a bed in front of the tree. Doffing their robes, she lay on her back. He made love to her as he did, to her mind first, whispering words of love, then to her body, all of her sensitive places, until she was way past the moon in ecstasy. She tried to be quiet, but her climaxes consumed her, and she couldn't still her cries.

Afterward, they crept back to bed, to resume a normal night's sleep.

Early Christmas morning, she set out the few presents for Dad and Norman under the tree. She expected nothing, especially after her surprise at Harry Winston.

Back in bed, half laying on sleeping Norman, she mused on Norman's surprise as she drifted toward sleep.

I was surprised by his proposal.

She touched her ring, running her fingers over the stones.

He loves me, I know it, and what he did is who he is, a lavish giver.

She sighed as her thoughts warmed her heart, resonating with her love for him.

Walking with him, arm in arm, with a ring on my finger fills me with joy to know his intention to love me above all others. He has said so; now I have proof in diamonds and sapphires.

Rising by agreement, about nine, they enjoyed coffee and some marvelous pastries that Arthur arranged to be delivered. Christie saw a huge box under the tree. Knowing it was not from her, she looked at it, and it was for her. Neither Dad nor Norman would confess. After their breakfast, they opened their gifts. Dad insisted Christie open hers first. Half an acre of paper later, she found one of those magnificent coffee machines that made everything, from both of them, so neither lied when they said that individually they didn't give it to her. She hugged Dad and then Junior, saying, "How will we get it back on the plane?"

Junior looked at her quizzically, and then she said, "Well, duh, we have our own plane."

Dad laughed and said, "I think it will be no problem."

Dad was next. She bought him an elegant red and gold tie, which was rolled into a coffee cup lettered in gold, "World's Greatest Dad." He hugged her in thanks, insisting the mug be put to immediate use.

Junior also received a mug, letter as "World's Greatest Husband." She looked sheepishly between them, shrugging, "I bought it in Petoskey and hoped it would be true."

Both Normans laughed. They ate more pastries with coffee, asking Dad what Christmas was like when he was little. They talked for an hour, reliving their favorite Christmas memories.

Christie announced, "Okay, men, we have work to do if we're going to eat our dinner."

Gathering around the island, she took food from the fridge with three pages of instructions. They organized the food around Arthur's advice, and she made preparation assignments. Seeing the roast, she exclaimed, "This is the most beautiful roast I've ever seen."

"Arthur knows where to buy food," Dad said.

Junior added, "That's true for sure."

Arthur gave them a timing chart when each dish would start to cook to have them all come out at the same time. Christie loved how organized he was.

They worked, laughed, told stories, drank Gewürztraminer, bumped into each other, and had a blast. Dad said, "Had I known that cooking was this much fun, I'd have been in here with Arthur as he made meals for me."

Christie laughed, and Junior added, "It's fun because we're a family, working together."

Dad lifted his wine glass and said, "Here, here."

They set the table together, Junior setting some silverware upside down so Christie would scold him when she fixed it. Standing back, they surveyed an elegant table, candles, and all. The buzzer rang, and Christie consulted the instructions, taking the meat out to rest, then finishing the sauces for the vegetables. She marveled when it all seemed to be ready at the same time. Arthur was a genius.

Dad carried the roast to the table on a platter with a carving set. Norman dished up the sides adding spoons, and Christie put sauces into bowls adding ladles. Their meal lay before them, and Dad said, "We have to give thanks for all this."

He spoke a marvelous prayer, wrapping all the recent events into it, finally thanking God for their food. Junior and Christie held hands as he prayed. Both were moved by the summary that he gave of their lives and the joy they had by being together.

Thanks given, they set upon the food, a feast for a king. Everything was so savory that it was hard to stop, and they all ate too much, retiring to the sofa to digest before the cherry pie. Arthur had made it himself, from his secret recipe.

Dad had some videos of Junior when he was small, transcribed to DVD, and he played a few of them. Christie thought he was so cute. She would poke his ribs at a particularly funny part.

They ate pie and Dad said, "I have a thought about a wedding. I think you should have it at the Plaza. That hotel could create a fairy tale wedding. The out-of-town guests could stay there, so it's convenient for them. The group of them could visit New York sights before and after the wedding before they go home. I'd send a jet to get them, two jets if need be. It would be fun to have a grand celebration of you two."

Christie looked at Junior, saying, "We haven't talked about a wedding. I don't have many friends, a few. My brother and his family live in Jacksonville."

Junior said, "We have lots of friends and could easily fill the place."

Laughing, she said, "It will be like *My Big Fat Greek Wedding*, one side filled and the other empty."

Dad offered, "We could alternate the entering people, one side and then the other."

Junior laughed and said, "Good idea."

He looked at Christie and said, "Do you want that?"

"I wish my mother were here to help me. I don't know what to do, especially for a big wedding, a fancy one." Tears formed in her eyes.

Dad came to her rescue, looking at Norman. "Junior, we need to introduce Christie to my mother-in-law, Agnes, your grandmother. She's a spry eighty-four, would absolutely love to help you, and will do a bang-up job at it as well. It would invigorate her to plan such an event."

"Dad, that's a fantastic idea. I've not seen her in a while."

"Let me call her to see if she can come for left-overs tomorrow. Christie, you'll love her."

Dad hit one button on his phone. Christie asked Junior, "Dad has her on speed-dial?"

"She would have it no other way. Just wait till you meet her."

Dad said, "Agnes, it's so good to hear your voice."

Christie could faintly hear a woman's voice from the phone, but it was indistinct.

"I was wondering if you could come to visit me and Junior and his fiancée, Christie, tomorrow for lunch. We have marvelous left-overs."

Agnes responded.

"Yes, she's a wonderful girl, a lot like Maggie. You'll love her as I do. She's like a daughter to me already."

Christie's eyes turned liquid at his words, and Norman stroked her arm to comfort her.

"You have nothing to eat and would love to come. Wonderful. We'll see you at noon, then? I'll send a car for you at eleven. See you then."

Christie said, "It sounds like I'll be meeting the queen. Is she that regal?"

Dad's head wagged as he said, "Well, yes, and no. She can be regal if she wants to be or needs to be. She wields great power in the business world, though no one would ever know. She reads the Wall

Street Journal every day, front to back. But she can be as gentle as a kitten when she wants to be. You'll see her kitten side unless someone gets in her way, then the queen emerges and parts the ocean."

"She sounds like a great ally in crafting a wedding."

Dad said, "Oh, yeah. She'll build a fairy tale for you, pumpkins into carriages if you want."

"Really? I can't wait to meet her."

Chapter 18

Christie

Right at noon, there was a rap on the door. Dad answered it, and an old woman entered, splendid in appearance, regal in demeanor; she had a presence about her, an aura. Christie felt she needed to curtsy to her. She said to Dad, "I hear there's a new addition to the fam?"

"Yes, Christie Yaeger, a delightful young woman with many talents. Come in and meet her. She'll remind you of Maggie."

Norman whispered in her ear, "Don't be afraid of her. She'll love you."

She walked up to Norman and Christie, looking at him first, saying, "Chose a woman, at last, did you? And not a New York girl, glad to hear it. They're too snooty and fake."

"Yes, Grandmother. My love is Christie Yaeger," Junior gesturing to Christie.

Her gaze shifted to Christie, and she scanned her body from head to toe.

"Clothes from Saks?"

"Yes, ma'am."

With a big smile and sparkling eyes, she said, "Don't ma'am me. Call me either Grandma or Agnes."

Her back straight, eyes flitting to Junior, she said, "Norman said that maybe I should address you like the queen."

A huge laugh came from her, bigger than what should from her petite body. "He should say that because I can be if I want to. But, to you, I'm Grandma."

Christie's expression melted at her words, and she said, "Thank you. My parents and grandparents have all passed."

"I'm glad to serve in their stead. You're beautiful, by the way. Those clothes highlight your body well. Now, let me see your rock."

Christie grinned, held her hand out, and Agnes inspected her ring, nodding in approval as she touched the stones.

"Harry Winston does good work. It should come with a necklace and earrings, right?"

"Yes, how did you know?"

"I can tell their work anywhere, and they like sets, it ups the price. They have a flair that no one else has. Can I see your set?"

Excited to show off her pieces, she said, "Yes, let me put them on for you."

She whizzed to the bedroom, retrieved her set from their boxes, and returned to Agnes chatting with Junior. She stood before Agnes for inspection, back straight, face forward.

Agnes regarded her, touching the necklace stones and said, "Ah, yes. Nicely done. Sapphires, right?"

"Yes, ma'am. I mean, yes, Grandma."

Agnes smiled, patted her hand, and said, "Christie, we'll get along very well."

Agnes took her hand and walked toward the table, set with the food already out, ready for them. Arthur stood in the kitchen, ready to serve. Agnes saw him and said, "Merry Christmas, Arthur. Are you well?"

"Yes, ma'am, very well, my family too. And you?"

"Glad to hear it, and I'm well, but not enough energy for the day. Did you make this dinner?"

"No, ma'am. Christie and the men did. I supplied the ingredients and a bit of instruction to help them."

Agnes turned to Christie, regarding her, and said, "You have hidden talents. Junior told me that you're smart, inventive, good with a computer, and have ideas about business opportunities. A man needs his wife's ideas. You did up his presentation with a flourish, selling the client on the opportunity. Glad to hear it. I see more of my Maggie in you. You know, there are whispers about you all over town."

"Really? Whispers? About me? All over town?"

"Yes. They see a woman with Norman and Junior, and they don't know her. It makes them upset, especially when you look like them."

Christie took her words as a huge encouragement. She never thought of herself as being a possible talk of New York. Her heart swelled like a balloon.

Sitting, they passed the food.

As they ate, Dad said, "Agnes, I want you to craft a wedding for Junior and Christie, at the Plaza. I'll fly in her guests and put them up there. Our guests will be local, probably, a few from out of town."

Agnes regarded them, especially Christie, and said, "So, you want a fairy tale wedding, pumpkins into carriages, mice into horses?"

Christie nodded.

Agnes laughed and added, "You'll be the talk of the town, and no one will know you, only me. I love it. They'll be falling all over each other to get to you."

Christie's eyes widened, and she said, "Really?"

"Of course. Junior is off the market, and they don't know who nabbed him. They see him with an unknown woman, and they wonder who she is, salivating for the gossip. They won't know either until I choose to unveil you. I love it. They'll be like sharks in a feeding frenzy."

To Christie, she sounded like the queen now or even the Good Witch of the South, half expecting to see a magic wand in her purse.

Agnes looked at Christie, asking, "How soon do you want it to happen?"

"How fast can it happen?"

"Good question. I'd think we can be ready by April if I put some fire under them."

In her mind, Christie pictured blow torches hung on their backsides with Agnes cackling.

"That would be wonderful, but I don't want to put people out."

"Oh, honey, you'd not put them out, just get them off their butts and work for a change. They have it too easy. But you'll have to work too. I'll need you here from time to time, to select or approve things. Norman will send the jet, of course, though we can do some by phone. You need to be hands-on for certain things."

Dad nodded. Christie thought of Karen's words about money and how it made things happen. She thought about Agnes, how she prospered once Maggie married Norman.

I've shared some of my business ideas with Norman—never had the resources to act on them. Maybe they could come to fruition in a similar way?

The food was finished, and their conversation as well. Agnes had what she needed and had work to do, but turned to Junior asking, "Can she stay one more day? There's a dress designer, Mark, who I'm sure needs something to do two days after Christmas. He probably let everyone go until after the First, and he'll be pacing and bored, so we'll pay him a visit tomorrow."

She turned to Christie. "Say, at ten? I'll make the arrangements. Norman, send a car for me at nine, would you?"

"Of course."

"And I'll call the Plaza manager. We're old buddies, and I'll see what's available."

A smiling Christie nodded and said, "Grandma, thank you so much."

Agnes looked at Christie with a wink and a wry smile, before she said, "My dear, it's easy when you have a magic wand."

Christie looked at Norman with wide eyes, as if she was telling the truth. He laughed, and Dad said, "You think she doesn't."

Agnes laughed as she walked to the door holding Christie's hand.

"Norman says that you're Junior's equal in every way but money, and I believe it. Christie, your dinner was superb. That, added to all your other talents, I'm sure you'll make Junior a wonderful wife, a lifetime partner."

Christie looked at her, eye to eye, and said, "I think so."

"I know so, a lot like my Maggie was for Norman."

With that, she was out the door.

*****

Christie

Agnes and Christie met with Mark the next day. He stood them before an enormous book of dress designs. Christie never imagined so many existed. Mark circled her, adjusted her posture, pulled gently on her clothes, assessing her.

He asked, "Do you like this outfit?"

"Yes, I do."

"From Saks?"

"Yes, how do you know?"

"I can tell their clothes by the look and cut. Usually, they do good work."

Moving to the book, he parted the pages like Moses parted the Red Sea.

"Start here and see if anything resonates with you."

Mark paced as Agnes and Christie turned pages and examined gowns on beautiful women. Fifty-four pages in, they saw it—simple, but elegant, off-white with lace. Christie could see herself in that gown.

Agnes pointed and said, "That's the one. I can picture you in it already."

"Norman will love me in it."

Touching her cheek, Agnes assured her, "Dearie, Norman loves you in anything you wear. I suspect he loves you in your birthday suit as well. But this will look good on you."

Christie blushed at Agnes's forwardness.

Mark peered between them, saying, "Oh yes. I like that one. It will fit you like a glove and show off all your assets marvelously."

Agnes turned to Mark, saying, "Settled. Put the bill on my account. I'll settle up with Norman."

"Of course."

Christie marveled that Agnes had an account with a high-end dress designer.

Do people with money have accounts everywhere?

"How soon can it be ready, and when does she need to come for a fitting."

"We should be ready at the end of February for a first fitting. The wedding is in April?"

"I hope so, but I need to talk to the Plaza manager. Work, based on that, and I'll let you know a firm date."

Mark said, "Let me get some measurements." Christie stood on the podium as he measured her and made notes. The fact that a wedding was really happening settled on her more.

They exited to the limo. During the ride, Agnes put her through the inquisition about what her colors should be, the cake flavor, who would be in the wedding party, and what she wanted them to wear. By the time she arrived at Dad's building, her head spun with details.

"Grandma, I trust you with these details. If you like it, I will too. Let me know what I need to do."

A grinning Agnes nodded and said, "Christie, this will be fun and something for you to remember and tell your children about."

Junior and Dad met her at his door, and she told them that she had found a dress and that Agnes would work on all the details. Christie had entrusted her with those. They finished off the leftovers from Christmas, watched some more DVDs of Junior's childhood, and it was time for bed. Dad told them that the jet would be ready for them at one p.m., and they should leave here about noon.

Once in their room, Norman kissed her under her ear and whispered, "I want to make love to you tonight, our last night in the Big Apple."

Am I going to say no to a night of ecstasy? I don't think so. I'll never get headaches when Norman is with me.

She nodded, and he did his magic with her, taking her deep into ecstasy and then again about two a.m. Waking by ten to be ready to leave at noon was not easy.

On the way home, Norman asked, "Do you really love your house?"

"Yes. It's the only thing I have from my parents."

"Thought so. So, this is my idea. We do a major renovation and expansion of it to get ready for kids."

"You want kids?"

"Yes, several," he confirmed. His fingers ran through his hair. "Your lot is sizable, so we expand the garage for our cars, probably three or four."

"You want several kids, three or four?" Looking down, she imagined not being able to see her feet when she was pregnant.

"Yes, several. We'll live above the office while the renovation is happening."

"Will you love me when I'm big and fat and pregnant?"

"Of course, I will. You're carrying a baby, our baby. I'll love you and the baby. And, then, when the renovation is done, we'll move into your house, and mine will be either a guest house or more office."

"I might be really big because my mother was with me. I saw a picture of her just before she delivered me."

"I'll love you, however you are. What do you think of my plan?"

"Ummm. What plan? The plan for kids?"

"The plan I just told you, for your house."

"You told me about a plan for my house? I thought it was for kids?"

"No, for renovating your house?"

"I only heard your plan about kids, to have several of them, and that you'd still love me when I was big and pregnant."

He laughed, slapping his knee, and they talked about kid plans and renovation plans all the way home, and other things too.

Chapter 19

Christie

Agnes brought Christie to New York three times, two for dress fittings and one to test everything for approval. Agnes chose well, and Christie loved it all—food, cake, flowers, decorations, everything. She showed her the ceremony venue and then for the reception, telling her how the rooms would be decorated. She had a picture of the carriage that would carry her and Dad to the Plaza from his building. It was magical.

Norman came with her to her first fitting, but she expelled him from the actual fitting with, "No fair seeing the bride before the wedding—bad luck."

Agnes unveiled her to the press as Norman's fiancée, in the Plaza's room where the ceremony would be held. The room was packed, reporters and gossip rag writers eagerly awaiting the latest bits of news from the Peale family.

Before the frenzy began, Agnes asked, "Do you have any skeletons in your closet."

Christie's brow wrinkled as she thought and said, "My father murdered my mother. He shot her five times and then himself. The police came and took James, who was ten, and me, I was six, away to a foster home."

Agnes waved it away as nothing. She would deal with that.

"Anything else?"

"No. I'm a nobody."

A serious Agnes looked her in the eye, pointing a crooked finger at her and said, "That's a total lie. You're about to become very much a somebody. You're marrying into our family. I know, because it happened to me. When Norman married my Maggie, my world opened, and I ran through the door. For you, by not having a sordid past, you'll avoid all the scrutiny and torture that the press deals out today. That's a blessing for anyone."

The photographers blinded her, and fortunately, she had to say nothing, just stand and smile at her fiancé's side as he addressed the crowd, holding her hand. She wore the red dress she found at Saks, two roses in her hand, with all her jewels, and when a woman reporter asked her where she got her jewelry, she said, head high, looking her square in the eye, "Harry Winston. My fiancé bought them for me." That said it all.

Agnes chose the big day to be April twenty-first. James and his family were thrilled beyond measure to be taken by private jet and a limo to the Plaza for the ceremony. A bigger jet brought Karen from Midway, then Norman's partners, the assistants, Mary and Tina, Samantha, Mable, and he and Christie from Petoskey. It was a party all the way to Teterboro Airport. Norman and Christie stayed with Dad; the rest went to the Plaza.

Wedding Day arrived. Arthur came to make snacks and help where he could. The press hounded everyone, especially Christie. Dad had four bodyguards around her to protect her and help her get through the crowds.

Christie expelled Norman from Dad's home. Karen and Samantha arrived to help her get ready. Agnes came by to inspect her and announced, "You look like an angel. I'm so proud of you. You remind me of my Maggie on her wedding day."

Agnes's eyes turned liquid, and Christie hugged her, saying, "Thank you so much for making all this happen. You made me Cinderella at the ball. Without you, I'm Cinderella, the housemaid."

Agnes patted her cheek. "Dearie, you were always Cinderella at the ball. I just waved my magic wand and made a few things happen to remind you of who you really are."

Samantha laughed at the image in her mind.

Right at twelve forty-five, Dad escorted Christie out of his building, through the gauntlet of photographers, kept at bay by police and six bodyguards, into the Cinderella carriage to take them to the Plaza.

The room was packed—317 guests. The wedding party was Karen, her maid of honor—and Samantha, then his partners, Ryan— his best man—and Edward. The wedding party assembled. Agnes would go down first as the Grandmother. Then the girls, then Christie and Dad. Christie gasped when she saw the room, clinging to Dad. To say it was magical was wholly inadequate—it was a fairy tale in full measure. The official stood with Norman and his groomsmen, awaiting the big moment.

Music played, and it sounded like a full pipe organ with all the stops open. The girls made their way to the front, followed by Dad and Christie with everyone standing.

As they walked, Dad whispered, "You know, I never had a daughter to give away, but in you, I found one." Both tried, unsuccessfully, to hold their emotions in check.

The question came, "Who gives this woman to this man?"

Dad rose to the occasion, his emotions somehow restrained, his voice ringing out clearly, "Her mother and her father would, were they here. In their stead, I do, with great pleasure."

Christie lost it, sobbing, tears running down her cheeks, her whole body shaking, but everyone waited until she regained her composure. Norman held her hands, whispering to her, comforting her. Dad stepped to his place in the front row, and the ceremony proceeded.

Vows were spoken, deep intentions of commitment and rings were exchanged, endless symbols of their love and devotion to each other. In the end, Norman and Christie Peale were introduced to the audience to cheers and applause. Three photographers and two video guys captured everything.

The reception was a huge party of celebration with food, dancing, introductions, and stories about the bride and groom from the wedding party. It lasted past midnight, though the new husband and wife left for their room about ten-thirty. The plan was for three nights at the Plaza, then back to Petoskey for two weeks, then to a 28-day cruise from San Diego to Hawaii and the French Polynesian islands.

The new couple was ready for their new life, eager to tackle what came at them.

The End

For news on upcoming books, free goodies, and other stuff,

please sign up on my contact page.

https://merrygoodman.com/contact-merry/

Don't miss the next book in the *Love Me Forever* series coming soon!!

About the Author

Hi!   I'm Merry Goodman.

I love to write contemporary and inspirational romance short stories and novellas, thirty-minute to two-hour reads, sweet romances with some sizzle in them. They warm your heart and give flight to your imagination. For someone who hated English in High School and University, I sometimes wonder how I got here.

I've had animals on four acres: horses, dogs, cats, one named Max, who emitted horrific gas if hugged, chickens, and some hilarious ducks, Indian Runners, which ran rather than waddled. Now, in the city, I have only four houseplants and a ginormous silver maple tree outside for squirrels and birds.

This is the first book in the series: *Love Me Forever*. They are individually available on Amazon; search for them with my name, Merry Goodman.

I have books in three series.

Love at First Sight: These stories are short reads, clean and sweet tales of finding love instantly, letting it simmer, and then a proposal. They could be rated PG.

You Found Me and Loved Me: These stories are a bit longer, ninety-minute to two-hour reads. They are sweet and almost-clean, just a little more sizzle. They could be rated PG-13.

Love Me Forever: These contemporary stories are longer than my other tales, two-hour reads, and have more sizzle in them—R rated.

I hope you enjoy reading them as I did writing them.

Thanks so much for reading my tale of love and connection. I would love to hear from you. If you enjoyed this book, I would love a review if you would be so kind.

Sign up for Merry's newsletter, free goodies, news, and other stuff:

merrygoodman.com/contact-merry/

Visit Merry's website:

www.merrygoodman.com

Merry's Twitter account is:

@MerryGoodman6

Visit Merry on Facebook:

Facebook.com/Merry-Goodman-Romances

Merry's Amazon Author Page is:

Amazon Author Page

You can email me:

author.merry.goodman@gmail.com

Quick reads by Merry Goodman
Series: Love at First Sight

Recipe for Love

The Neighbor

Bad Date Redeemed

Can Ice Cream Bring Me Love?

North to Alaska

Love at First Sight, Box Set

This box set is a collection of the above five stories.

It is available in both eBook and paperback formats.

Part-Time Worker, Full-Time Lover

The *Love at First Sight* series continues with:

Girls' Weekend

The Christmas Surprise

Two Lemons Turned into Sweet Lemonade

First Comes Baby, Then Comes Love

Lakeside Lovers

Brought Together by Our Cats

Love at First Sight, Volume 2

This box set is a collection of the above six stories.

It is available in both eBook and paperback formats.

The *Love at First Sight* series continues with:

Evenings at La Grolla

We're in This Together

Longer Stories by Merry Goodman

Series: You Found Me and Loved Me

Found in Acapulco

Found at the Messiah

Encounter in Nashville

Found by Love a Second Time

You Found Me and Loved Me

This box set is a collection of the above four stories.

It is available in both eBook and paperback formats.

The series continues with:

Take My Breath Away

Stories with more Sizzle by Merry Goodman

Series: Love Me Forever

Part-Time Worker, Full-Time Lover

Batting One Thousand

Lovers on the Lido Deck

Wild Goose Island

Made in the USA
Middletown, DE
23 February 2021

34258875R00102